# The Last Healer

By Charles Huss

For my wife, Rose, because she said so. Also, because she makes me happy, which is really the primary goal in life.

# Chapter 1

The hospital at Ellis Island seemed more crowded with patients than usual as Head Nurse Elizabeth Young signed in to start her shift. "Good morning, Betty," came a familiar voice behind her.

She turned to see her fellow nurse and friend, Mary White, standing behind her. "Good morning, Mary," she said. "It looks like you had a busy night."

"We sure did. A ship arrived late yesterday, filled with refugees from the war," she said. "Most were from Croatia, and many were in bad shape."

"Why does this keep happening?" Betty asked. "We are sixteen years into the twentieth century and still herd people across the Atlantic like cattle. I mean, we have airplanes, automobiles, and even underwater boats, but we can't make ships designed to carry people safely and humanely across the ocean."

"I agree, Betty, but there is a war going on," Mary said. "These people escaped it. They are the lucky ones. Most of them, anyway."

"I know, Mary, but it still seems wrong. I suppose we should consider ourselves lucky that we are not sending our men over there to die."

"We are lucky, Betty, but some days feel less lucky than others," Mary said. "We lost a pregnant mother last night. It was heartbreaking. Fortunately, we saved her baby, but he is weak. Doctor Roberts thinks his chances of survival are very low."

"That's terrible," Betty said. "What about the father?"

Mary just looked at Betty, and Betty understood that the father didn't survive the war.

Betty shook her head slowly and said, "I want to see the baby."

"I don't think that would be a good idea," Mary said. "He'll be lucky if he survives the next couple of days. The pediatric nurse will take care of him. I know you. I think it would be best for you not to get involved."

"I'm the head nurse here, Mary. It's my job to get involved."

"Okay, but don't say I didn't warn you."

Betty followed Mary to the maternity section, where three babies were in bassinets. Mary pointed at the one to the far left. "There he is," she said.

"Oh, my. He is so little."

"The doctor thinks he is about nine weeks premature," Mary said. "Combine that with the extreme stress and poor nutrition of the mother. Well, I wouldn't get too attached."

Betty looked at the chart and saw the mother's name was Eva Novak. "Has anyone named the child yet?" she asked.

"No. Things have been pretty crazy," Mary said. "We found a letter on the mother, but it needs to be translated."

"A letter? Where is it?"

"Under the chart, I think."

Betty lifted the chart and found the letter. It had several fold lines across it and was in a language she didn't understand. She folded the letter and put it in her pocket. "You've had a long night, Mary. Go home and get some rest. I'll handle it from here."

"I know what you're thinking, Betty. I worry you will get your heart broken, but I also know anything I say will fall on deaf ears."

"I appreciate your concern, Mary, but don't worry. I will be fine."

"I hope so," Mary said before turning to leave.

Betty did her rounds that morning and soon found an elderly Croatian woman who spoke English well. She looked at her chart and said, "How are you feeling today, Mrs., uh…"

"Mia," she said. "You can call me Mia."

"Forgive me, Mia. I've never been good with names."

"Don't worry, Dear. It took me a while to get used to English names."

"Well, I'm very pleased to meet you, Mia. How are you feeling this morning?

"I am feeling much better this morning. I think I am ready to get out of here."

"The doctor will be in later to check on you, but I see no reason to keep you here longer than necessary," Betty said. "While you are here, I would like to ask for your help with something."

"Of course. I can't imagine how I can help you, but I will try."

Betty took out the letter and asked, "Will you translate this letter for me?"

The woman took the letter from Betty and read it. When she did, the smile disappeared from her face. "There was a pregnant girl on the ship that I was on. Did she write this?

"Yes, she did."

"Is she okay?"

Betty shook her head slowly and said, "I'm afraid she didn't make it."

The woman closed her eyes for several seconds and then wiped away tears with her fingers. "She was a lovely young lady," she said. "Why would God spare an old woman like me but take such a beautiful young soul?

"I don't know," Betty said. "Pregnancy can be hard on a woman, but the baby is alive. Barely. That is why I need your help to read the letter."

The woman looked at the letter again and started to read, "My name is Eva Novak. My husband was killed in the war, and I am alone. I am very weak and don't know if I will make it. We will arrive in America soon, and I will try to hold on for the baby. My life is not important, but my child means everything to me. Whatever happens to me, please save my baby. If it is a boy, please call him Josip, after his father. If it is a girl, please call her Ana, after my mother. Please help my baby." She again wiped tears from her eyes when she finished.

Betty was choked up after hearing the letter. She quickly thanked the woman and left for fear of having an emotional outburst in front of her. She returned to the nursery and wrote "Josip Novak" on the baby's chart. She continued her duties but checked on the baby every hour or so.

As the days turned to weeks, Josip became stronger and stronger and was ready to leave the hospital to become a ward of the state. By then, the bond between Josip and Betty was as strong as the one between Betty and her own children. After discussing the matter with her husband and their three children, who were all in their teens, they decided that little Josip would be a welcome member of the Young family.

# Chapter 2

"I don't think the lighting is good enough here," Katie said. "Maybe we should shoot it inside."

"The lighting is fine," said her friend and camerawoman, Ashley.

"What about the wind? Do you think it's too much?"

"I think it's perfect. Your long, dark, silky hair is gently swaying with the breeze. What man wouldn't find that sexy?"

"Maybe it's too cold. What if I shiver when I talk?"

"It's thirty degrees. You can handle that. What has gotten into you today?"

Katie sighed and said, "I just feel like I have been stuck in this job for too long. If I want a promotion, everything I do has to be perfect."

"Nobody's perfect, Katie."

"Especially people who don't get promoted," Katie said.

"Why are you suddenly worried about that now?"

"I don't know. I guess because my thirtieth birthday is on Sunday. I feel like I'm in a rut."

"You're turning thirty? That's great. Happy birthday, Katie. I wish you had told me earlier."

"I don't exactly want to celebrate turning the big three oh."

"Sure you do. A birthday is a time to celebrate. Besides, age is just a number."

"Yes, and numbers are what people use to measure things, and by my measurement, I should be further ahead in my career. Let's talk about this later, Ashley. Right now, I want to get this over with."

Katie walked over to the man she was scheduled to interview, and Ashley said, "Okay, we're rolling in three, two, one, go."

"Hello, Milwaukee. This is Katie Knight in front of Bill's Hot Dogs. We are here today with Jimmy Smith, winner of this year's first and perhaps greatest hot dog eating contest in the city. Jimmy put down an impressive 56 hot dogs in ten minutes. Tell me, Jimmy, how do you feel?"

"Uh, full."

"I can believe that, Jimmy. So, what did you do to prepare for this contest?"

"Uh, I ate a lot of hot dogs."

"That's great, Jimmy. Thanks for your lovely insights into the world of professional hot dog eating. That's all we have time for today, so back to the studio."

Katie handed her microphone to Ashley and asked, "Why do I do this? I got into this profession to do serious journalism, not to interview brain-dead hot dog eaters. This job needs to change, or I need to develop a new plan for my life."

"Have you talked to Brad about this?" Ashley asked.

"Brad? No. Brad and I are over."

"What? You two broke up? This is my shocked face," Ashley said as she looked at Katie with her mouth hanging open.

"Stop," Katie said, laughing.

"So, what happened this time?"

"He booked a nice room at a ski resort up north for my birthday this weekend but backed out at the last minute. He said he has too much work to do."

"He's a slip-and-fall lawyer. What could possibly be so important?

"That's what I said. I told him I couldn't be with a man who put his job first and me second."

"I don't blame you. If I had more notice, I would love to take Brad's place, but we are taking the kids to Chicago to visit John's parents this weekend. Why don't you go there by yourself? You can do a little skiing, a little relaxing, and maybe you will meet a handsome stranger who will sweep you off your feet.

"Yeah, right. Like that's going to happen."

"Are you kidding? Look at you. You have a beautiful face, and I would kill to have a body like you have."

"Stop. You have no reason to be envious. I see the way men look at you."

"I'm thirty-five years old with two kids and a body that shows it. Men look at me because my boobs are too big."

"They look at you because you are attractive. You look like Barbie with your blonde hair and big boobs."

"If I were Barbie, I'd have a twenty-inch waist. That's not me."

"I see what you are doing," Katie said, "but you will not make me feel better about myself by putting yourself down."

"Just take my advice. Go away for the weekend. You'll feel better on Monday."

"Well, I suppose that might not be a bad idea. I could use a little time away to relax and unwind."

"There you go," Ashley said. "Maybe when you return on Monday, you will have a whole new perspective."

"It's unlikely a weekend away will change my life, but who knows? Anything's possible, right?"

"That's right. The tiniest change could alter your life forever."

"We'll see," Katie said.

***

When Katie got home, she pulled the reservation out of the trash. She threw it away after her fight with Brad, but now she had second thoughts. She looked at it for a long minute, pulled her suitcase out of the closet, and started packing. It was her thirtieth birthday, and come Hell or high water, she would enjoy it.

When Katie finished packing her bag, she heard her cell phone ringing. She checked the number. It was her mother. "Hi, Mom."

"Hi, dear. We haven't heard from you this week, so I thought I would call to see if you are okay."

"I'm okay, Mom."

"Just okay? That doesn't sound good."

"Brad and I broke up."

"I'm so sorry to hear that, Dear."

"It's fine, Mom. I don't think we were right for each other anyway."

"Relationships can be complicated, Katie."

"How did you know Dad was the one for you?"

"I'm afraid that isn't something I can put into words. It is a feeling. When the right man comes along, you will know."

"I don't know if the right man exists, Mom."

"You're just feeling down right now, but the right man is out there. Believe me. Since you will be free on your birthday, why don't you come home for the weekend? We can celebrate here."

"I appreciate that, Mom, but I have a reservation at a ski resort that Brad and I were supposed to visit. I think that is a good place for me to go and de-stress for a while."

"That's a wonderful idea, Katie. These things take time, and I know you will be fine. In fact, I think it is best not to waste too much time on the wrong guy. Who knows? Maybe you will run into Mr. Right on your little getaway."

"I'll be thirty on Sunday, Mom. I doubt it will happen over the weekend if I haven't run into Mr. Right in thirty years."

"I guess we'll see, Dear. You enjoy your weekend, and if you change your mind, we would love to see you."

"Thanks, Mom. I'll call you when I get there tomorrow."

"Okay, Katie. I love you."

"I love you too, Mom."

Katie hung up the phone and sat on the sofa, mulling over her future. Maybe becoming an investigative reporter was just a pipe dream. Perhaps she should return home and find a man to marry before she's too old. They could have a couple of kids and maybe buy a house with a white picket fence. It then occurred to her that these were the thoughts of someone who had given up, and she was not ready to give up.

# Chapter 3

The next morning, Katie put her suitcase in the car and entered the resort's address into the car's GPS. She didn't own skis, which was probably just as well since they wouldn't fit in her little Mini Cooper. She figured she could just rent them when she got there. She wasn't even sure if she wanted to ski. Perhaps sitting by the fire with a good book was all she needed. After all, she had only skied once in her life ten years ago and would probably need to learn all over again.

The temperature had dropped a bit since yesterday, and she was starting to see snow flurries. It was nothing unusual for January, so she thought nothing of it. After about an hour of driving, the wind picked up, and the snow started falling hard, significantly diminishing visibility.

Exiting the highway, she found herself on a narrow, winding road. After several miles, she came upon a snowplow, which she was able to follow for several more miles until her GPS instructed her to turn down another street. This street was barely wide enough for two cars, and Katie wondered if her GPS was malfunctioning. Due to the snow, it was difficult to determine the road's edge. She looked down at the map to see where she was. When she looked up, she saw a figure in front of her and slammed on the brakes. It was too late. The figure bounced off the hood of the car and slammed into the windshield before rolling off the driver's side and onto the street.

"Oh, my God!" Katie screamed and quickly got out of the car. The body was lying face down in the snow. She gently turned it over and saw it was a young man. His eyes were closed, and he was bleeding from a gash on his forehead. She put her ear against his mouth and could hear a slow, gurgling breath. At least he was alive.

She got back into her car and retrieved her phone. She dialed 911, but nothing happened. She had no signal. "Shit!" she said.

She went back outside to check on the young man whose eyes were now open. It seemed he wanted to speak, but nothing came out. Instead, he just pointed. Katie looked in the direction he was pointing and, through the snow, could barely make out a small cabin about a hundred yards away.

"Okay, I'll get you help," Katie said.

"No!" the man was able to get out. "Take me."

Katie looked at the cabin and said, "It's too far. I don't have the strength."

"Help me up."

"What?"

"Help me up. Drive me."

"That's crazy. I could hurt you worse by moving you."

"That's my cabin," he said in a low voice. "There's nobody there. Help me up. You won't hurt me."

Katie had her doubts, but she helped the man sit up. "The left side is okay," the man said.

She went to his left side and knelt so he could put his arm around her. She then used all her strength to pull the man to his feet. He hopped on one leg to the other side of the car. Katie opened the door and helped him sit down. He couldn't pull his legs inside, so she left the door open and got into the driver's seat.

She drove up the driveway, but her wheels spun in the snow. She tried to ease on the accelerator gently. After a few attempts, the wheels finally grabbed, and the car moved forward. She made it to within forty feet of the front door but could go no further. She decided it was close enough and raced around to the other side of the car. She helped the man to his feet, and they hobbled to the front door. It was painstakingly slow.

When they reached the door, Katie opened it and helped him inside. The cabin was small. Everything was in one room. Something was cooking on the stove, and the smell reminded Katie of her mom's chicken soup. Her mom would make it whenever Katie was sick.

Inside the cabin to the right was a small kitchen and eating area with a table big enough for only two people. Straight ahead at the back of the cabin, a fire burned in the fireplace. To the left, against the front window, was a sofa, and further to the right was a small double bed. Between the sofa and bed was a nightstand. On the other side of the bed stood a dresser. Beyond that, in the far corner, was a small closet.

Katie helped the man hobble to the bed and then helped him remove his coat. She could see his right arm was severely bruised and probably broken. She lifted his shirt and saw the entire right side of his chest was purple. She wasn't about to take his pants off to check his legs, but she was sure his right leg was probably broken, too.

"Where's your phone?" Katie asked. "I need to call an ambulance."

"I have no phone," the man said.

"You have no phone? What about a cell phone?"

"I don't have a cell phone, either," the man said.

"Who doesn't have a phone these days?" Katie asked, frustrated.

"That would be me," the man said.

"I need to get help for you. Tell me where to go. I'm a bit lost, and my GPS is confused."

"There's quite a snowstorm out there," he said. "You won't make it very far. Don't worry about me. I only need rest. I'll be fine."

"Don't give me that macho crap. You won't be fine. You probably have multiple broken bones and possibly internal bleeding. You need a hospital."

"I need rest. You are welcome to stay here until the storm dies down."

Katie got up and went to the kitchen area and found paper towels. She took one off the roll, wet it, and put a small amount of soap on it. She returned and wiped the blood off the man's forehead. He had a three-inch cut that surprisingly had stopped bleeding.

"If you want, there is soup simmering on the stove," the man said. "Perhaps you can dish a little out for both of us."

Katie couldn't understand why this young man was so nonchalant about his injuries, but she could see no other course of action until the snow let up. She walked into the kitchen area and picked up the cover on the large pot simmering on the stove. She picked up a large spoon next to the pot, stirred the soup, and then picked up a spoonful to see what it was. It looked like chicken and vegetable soup.

"This is a lot of soup for one guy," Katie said.

"That will last me several days, maybe a week," the man said. "Bowls are above you and to the right. Spoons are in the drawer below the bowls."

Katie put soup in two bowls and added a spoon to each. She grabbed a couple of napkins, carried the bowls across the room, and set them down on the nightstand next to the bed. She pulled a chair next to the bed and started to spoon-feed the soup to the man, but he stopped her, saying, "No. Help me up."

"Are you sure?" Katie asked. "I don't mind feeding it to you. It doesn't make you less of a man to accept help."

"This has nothing to do with manliness," the man said. "I just think that I can do it myself."

"Okay," Katie said and helped him to sit up straight. She then put the soup bowl on his lap and handed him the spoon.

"By the way, my name's Katie."

"I'm Joe. I'm very pleased to meet you, although I wish it were under better circumstances. Forgive me, but I can't shake your hand right now."

"I am so sorry, Joe. The snow was falling so hard that I didn't see you until it was too late. What were you doing on the street in such bad weather anyway?"

"It seems I chose the wrong time to check my mailbox."

Joe picked up a spoonful of soup and spilled half of it on his chest before reaching his mouth. "I guess I'm not used to eating soup this way."

"Give me that," she said as she took his bowl of soup. She wiped his chest with a napkin and began feeding him the soup. "I don't want to hear any complaining from you about this."

When Joe had finished his soup, Katie set the bowl down and began eating her soup. "This is very good," she said.

"Thank you. It's an old family recipe."

"You look too young to have picked up old family recipes. Most people your age are busy partying or off at college. Where are your parents, by the way? Do you live here alone?"

"Well, I'm older than you think, and yes, I do live here alone. The rest of my family is not far from here. They manage the Three Eagles Ski Resort."

"You're kidding. That's where I was headed when I got lost. I have a reservation there this weekend."

"Well, maybe by tomorrow morning, we can get you there, and you can enjoy at least half of your weekend," Joe said.

"Don't be silly. As soon as the roads are passable, I am getting to a phone to call you an ambulance."

"I would prefer that you didn't do that, Katie. Just let my family know, and they will care for me."

Katie looked at him for several seconds and asked, "Are you in some kind of trouble? Is that why you are hiding out in this cabin."

"No, I am not in trouble, and I am not hiding out. This has been my home for years."

"Years? You're what, twenty-three? Twenty-five? How many years have you lived here alone?"

Katie stood up, picked up the soup bowls, and said, "I'm sorry. I shouldn't have spoken to you like that." She then carried the bowls to the sink and washed them.

When she returned, Joe said, "There was no need to apologize, Katie. You were well within your rights to speak to me like that. I would probably feel the same way if I were in your position. I know my circumstances are unusual, and I don't blame you for being suspicious of me. I can only tell you that I am not a fugitive of the law nor a threat to you."

Katie looked at him momentarily and said, "You are not a threat to anyone right now. Let me help you lie down. You do need your rest."

Katie helped Joe lie down again, and he quickly fell asleep. She looked out the window at the snow coming down and worried that Joe might not survive until she could get help for him. She didn't think she could handle knowing she was responsible for a man's death.

She got up and looked around the cabin. She noticed the fire was burning low. She saw a few logs on a metal tray near the fireplace and added one to the fire.

Several photos hung on the walls. One caught her eye. It was a black-and-white photo of a man in an Army uniform. It looked like a World War Two era photo, but the man looked exactly like Joe. She thought it was probably his great-grandfather, but the resemblance was amazing, especially for being so many generations removed.

There were other family photos, too, that seemed odd to her. Some were black and white, but many were in color. Some of the color ones were faded like they were taken in the seventies or eighties. Many of the group photos showed a young man who looked exactly like Joe. Was it possible that some families had multiple generations that looked so similar? Katie thought it must be possible because she was seeing it here.

Near the bed was a small bookcase filled with old-looking books. There was The Great Gatsby, Moby Dick, Tom Sawyer and 1984. She took one out and flipped it open to the first page. It was a first edition of Call of the Wild. She sat down in a chair and started reading.

# Chapter 4

"Katie! Katie!"

Katie awoke suddenly. "What? What?" She had forgotten where she was. She looked around and realized she was still in Joe's cabin and had fallen asleep in the chair.

"Katie," the voice came again. She saw that Joe was awake and that it was nearly dark outside.

"Joe. Is everything okay?" she asked.

"Yes and no," he said. "I'm feeling a little better, but I need to pee."

She hadn't considered that and didn't quite know what to do about it. "Okay, sure. Let's see. What can I do?"

"Just help me up, please."

"No. Who knows how much damage I did the first time I moved you? We can't risk making you worse."

"It will be okay," Joe said. "I'm not going to pee in a cup, especially not in front of you. Trust me. I can do this."

Katie thought about it for a few seconds and said, "Okay, fine. Where's your bathroom?"

"There's an outhouse behind the cabin, but there is no need to go that far. Just get me out the front door."

Katie went to his side and helped Joe to sit up. She noticed the bruising on his right arm was almost gone. "What the hell!" she said and lifted his shirt to look at his chest. It looked almost normal.

"Should you be doing that on a first date?" Joe asked.

She looked at his forehead, and the cut was barely noticeable. "Nobody heals this quickly," she said. "Is this some kind of game? Did you throw yourself on my car on purpose? Are you trying to scam me?"

"I am not trying to scam you. Please, help me now, and I will try to explain everything."

Katie looked at him for several long seconds and then said, "Fine, but if you are trying to scam me, I will make sure everyone knows about it. I happen to be a news reporter for Channel 23 News."

"A reporter, huh?" Joe said. "Well, I guess I will just have to not scam you."

Katie helped put Joe's coat on, and then she put her coat on. She helped him out of the bed, and they hobbled to the front door. Katie noticed it was a little easier now than it was when she brought him into the house. She opened the front door and saw that the snow had slowed and was only coming down in flurries. The last remnant of daylight was disappearing behind the trees.

"I need you to stay with me and help hold me up," Joe said.

When he unzipped his pants and started to pee, Katie looked away, but the temptation was too great, and she had to sneak a peek. When he finished, he zipped up his pants, smiled, and said, "Did you like what you saw?"

Unfazed, Katie replied, "I've seen better."

"Ouch," Joe said as they hobbled back into the cabin.

Once Katie had Joe back in his bed, she said, "I have to pee too. I'll be back in a minute." She went around to the back of the cabin to the outhouse and found the simple act of peeing was the most unpleasant thing she had done in a long time, outside of breaking up with Brad. She wondered how people in the old days survived.

When she returned, she sat beside Joe and said, "Okay, spill it. What is going on here? And don't bullshit me. I can smell bullshit a mile away."

"To be honest, Katie, knowing you are a reporter means I can't trust you with my story," Joe said. "I have been perfectly happy living a life of privacy. If what I am gets out, I might as well kiss it all goodbye."

"You said you are not wanted by the police. I assume that means there is no danger of you going to prison, so how bad can it be?"

"There are different kinds of prisons, Katie."

"I get that. I feel like I'm in one now."

"Really? How so?" Joe asked.

"When I said I was a reporter, that was kind of stretching the truth. I am actually a 'news personality' who seems to have been placed in personal interest stories jail. I will be thirty years old tomorrow, and I can't get past doing stories about hot dog eating contests."

"Well, happy birthday. You look great for being over the hill," Joe said with a laugh.

"Laugh all you want," Katie said. "Someday, you will turn thirty, and then let's see how funny you think it is."

"I happen to be over thirty," Joe said.

"Shut the front door!" Katie said. "I don't believe it."

"It's true, Katie."

"Well, you look really good for over thirty. How old are you?"

"That is something I prefer not to talk about with a reporter, or a news personality, or whatever you are."

"I promise this will be completely off the record," Katie said. "I have no desire to bring more harm into your life than I already have."

"I'm sorry, Katie. I can't risk it."

"I have already seen some very unusual things here. If you don't tell me, my curiosity will force me to investigate, and that investigation will be on the record."

Joe thought about it and eventually said, "Okay, you win, but you must promise this stays between us."

"Of course, Joe. I promise I will not tell anyone your secret."

"Okay, get me a knife from the kitchen."

"A knife? What do you need a knife for?" Katie asked.

"Bring me a knife, and I will show you. Bring a paper towel, too."

Katie opened the silverware drawer and found a knife. She then pulled a paper towel off the roll and brought them both to Joe. He took the knife in his left hand, held up his right hand, and sliced it across the palm.

"Shit, Joe! What the hell's the matter with you?" Katie grabbed his right hand and dabbed the cut with the paper towel. "This is deep. You need a bandage."

"No!" he said and closed his fingers into a fist. "I only need rest. Tomorrow, you will see."

"See what? What will I see?"

Joe said nothing. His eyes were closed. Sensing she would not win this one, Katie said, "You really are something, Joe. I don't know whether to admire you or get you a psychiatrist."

Joe remained silent, so Katie decided to let him sleep. She picked up the book she was reading and settled into the sofa.

After about an hour, Katie put the book down and checked on Joe. He was still sleeping. She checked her phone, but still had no signal. She noticed the battery was low and needed to be charged. She figured she should bring her suitcase inside since she would be stuck there until morning. She put on her coat and went out to the car. She noticed that the snow had stopped and briefly considered getting in her car to try to make it to the ski resort, but she didn't know how the roads were or even exactly where she needed to go.

After dragging her suitcase inside, she opened it and removed her phone charger. She found an outlet beside the sofa and plugged her phone into it. She usually slept nude at home, but packed an oversized t-shirt just in case. She was glad she did. She stripped down to her panties and removed her bra before putting the t-shirt on. There was a blanket folded at the end of the sofa, so she opened it and covered herself as she lay on the sofa.

"Pink panties look very sexy on you."

Katie looked up and saw Joe's eyes were open. "Damn you, Joe. I thought you were sleeping."

"How could anyone sleep through all that racket you were making?"

"Did you like what you saw?"

"I've seen better."

"Go to sleep, Joe."

# Chapter 5

Katie awoke the next morning and noticed the sun shining through the window. She then saw Joe sitting up in bed. "Good morning, Sunshine," he said. "Happy birthday. I'm sorry, but I didn't have a chance to get you a gift."

Katie sat up on the sofa and then realized she was underdressed. She pulled the blanket up to cover herself. "Good morning, Joe," she said. "Thank you."

"Don't worry about covering up. I've already seen pretty much everything," Joe said with a smile.

"Joe, I've known you for less than a day, and I already want to kill you."

"You can try, but it didn't work yesterday," Joe said, smiling again.

"It appears I didn't damage your sense of humor. How are you feeling today?"

"Not a hundred percent, yet, but much better."

Realizing there was no point in being modest, Katie stood up and walked over to Joe. "Let me look at you," she said. She checked his right arm and saw no sign of injury. She pressed gently on his forearm and asked, "Does this hurt?"

"Yes, a little."

"A little? Like what on a scale from one to ten?"

"Maybe a three."

"That's incredible. Were you seriously hurt yesterday, or were you pulling my leg?"

"I was seriously hurt yesterday, Katie. This is no joke."

"Okay, what was your pain level yesterday?"

"At least an eleven. Getting hit by a car hurts like Hell."

Katie lifted his shirt and noticed his chest looked perfectly normal. She pressed her finger against his chest. "What does that feel like?"

"A two, I guess."

"I need to see your leg."

"If you want to get into my pants, Katie, just ask."

"Okay, Joe. May I get into your pants, please?"

"Never on a first date," Joe said, smiling again.

"The first date was yesterday," Katie said. "This would be a second date."

"In that case, by all means," he said and unbuttoned his jeans.

Katie helped pull the jeans down and noticed his right leg still had some bruising and redness, but nothing like she expected. She pushed on the front of his thigh muscle and noticed a slight cringe. "Did that hurt?" she asked.

"Yes, maybe a four or five."

"Apparently, you are not Superman, but a five is a lot better than an eleven," Katie said before helping to pull his pants back up.

"Now, you were going to tell me about your big secret."

Joe held up his right hand and opened it so Katie could see the palm. It was covered in dried blood. She went into the kitchen and wet a paper towel. When she returned, she wiped the blood off and saw just a hint of a cut. It looked like it happened a week ago.

"How can this be?" she asked. "I saw you slice your hand open."

"I healed myself last night," Joe said.

"What? You healed yourself? What do you mean?"

"I healed myself," Joe repeated. "That is why I needed rest. Rest is a time of healing."

"I've had plenty of rest after injuries, but never healed that quickly," Katie said.

"That is because your healing is unconscious. My healing is conscious."

"You mean you are able to think yourself better?"

"I never thought of it that way, but that would be pretty accurate. Think of it this way. When you stub your toe, you feel pain in your toe because your body has nerve endings there, but what about your heart, your lungs, or your liver? Can you feel those? Maybe you can if they become a serious problem, but for the most part, people don't feel what is happening inside their bodies. I do. Not only that, I can also direct resources to correct any problem that I detect."

Katie looked at him with disbelief and said, "Are you saying that if you had a tumor growing in your colon, you would not only know what and where it is, but you could also send hordes of white blood cells, or whatever, to eliminate it?"

"In the case of a tumor, I would cut off its blood supply, but you are essentially correct."

Katie took the paper towel in her hand and wiped Joe's forehead. The cut that she saw yesterday had healed almost entirely. "Okay, Joe. If I hadn't seen it with my own eyes, I would think you were lying to me. I just don't understand how this is possible?"

"I don't know, either," Joe said. "I didn't even realize I was different until I was almost ten years old. My father died of a heart attack. I couldn't understand why he let that happen. I asked my mother why he didn't heal himself. She looked at me like I had two heads and asked why I would ask such a ridiculous question. I realized then that I was different and tried to keep a low profile after that."

"Is your mother still alive?" Katie asked.

"I don't know how to put this in a way that would be believable to you, so I will just say it. My birth mother died the day I was born. My adoptive mother passed away in 1956, two months before my fortieth birthday."

"What?" Katie said. "Are you telling me you were born in, let's see, 1916?"

"That's right. My real father was killed in The Great War. My mother came to America as a refugee. In those days, trips across the Atlantic were difficult for the passengers. I suppose the trip was too much for her. She held on until the ship docked in New York. I assume she let go once she knew I had a chance at life. That was the third of October 1916."

"Holy shit!" Katie said. "That would make you over a hundred years old. You're a centenarian. A young centenarian, but still a centenarian. So does that mean those photos on the wall are pictures of you?"

"Some of them. Yes"

"Is that you in the Army uniform?"

"Yes, that is me. It's not my best photo. I wasn't sure if I should smile or look serious, so I ended up somewhere in the middle."

"I think you look very handsome in uniform," Katie said. "Were you in World War Two?"

"Yes. I joined the Army before the war started and ended up in North Africa as a combat photographer."

"I can't imagine what that was like. Were you ever injured over there?"

"Yes, I was. A grenade went off near me. I was hit with shrapnel in my legs and back. It was bad enough to hurt me, but not kill me. To be totally honest, I could have healed much faster, but that would have drawn too much unwanted attention to me. As a result, the Army sent me home to recuperate in the United States, which is possibly why I am still around today.

"Were you scared when you were over there?" Katie asked.

"Sometimes, yes. I think only fools have no fear. It wasn't fear, though, that made me hate being over there. War is a horrible thing, and my job was to document it. It's bad enough seeing death the first time, but photographing it so that you could relive it when the film is developed just got to be too much."

"I am so sorry you had to go through that, Joe."

"At least it is all in the past."

"Tell me. What is bad enough to kill you? Does someone have to take your head?"

"I'm not the Highlander, Katie. This is real life. I can die just like you. You might have killed me if you had hit me harder with your car. I might have frozen to death if you had left me outside in the cold. If whatever gets me doesn't kill me right away, I can heal myself, but I need rest and nutrition to do it effectively."

"What about aging? How do you stay young?" Katie asked.

"I wish I could explain it to you better, Katie, but it is like explaining color to someone who has only ever seen in black and white."

"Now that you mention that, I once did a story about a local woman who could see four primary colors instead of three like everyone else. It is an extremely rare genetic anomaly and only happens in women. If I remember correctly, the mutation comes in two or more pieces on the X chromosome, and both parents need to have a copy. Because women have two X chromosomes, the mutation is only possible with girls. Do you think you have something similar? Maybe your mutation is on the Y chromosome or some other combination."

"I never studied genetics, but now I wish I had. Do you think there might be more people out there like me?"

"It's possible," Katie said. "Maybe they are keeping a low profile like you are. Or maybe they are local to where your parents come from. Your real parents, I mean."

"Interesting," Joe said, "but I only know my mother came from Croatia. It's a fairly big country, and I don't know what part she came from. Since you are a reporter or at least a reporter wannabe, maybe you can help me research it."

"I would be happy to, Joe. Right now, though, I still feel I should get you some help."

"Don't worry. My grandson should be here soon. I help at the resort on the weekends or whenever they need help. I don't have a car, so I usually walk there, but after a big snowstorm like the one we had yesterday, he will come and get me."

"You knew he was coming all this time, and you didn't mention it," Katie complained.

"You didn't ask," Joe said. "Now help me get up and get dressed, please."

Katie helped Joe sit on the bed and retrieved a shirt and pants from the closet. He reached down and pulled a pair of socks and underwear from the nightstand beside the bed. He pulled off his shirt and put on the shirt Katie gave him. He then carefully stood up and dropped his pants. He asked Katie, "Would you like to turn around for this part?"

"Not particularly," Katie said. "You watched me get undressed, so it's only fair."

"Very well," Joe said before dropping his underwear. He stepped out of his pants and underwear and sat back on the bed. "I may need your help with this part. It's still painful to bend my leg.

Katie picked up his underwear and put his feet through the holes. She pulled it most of the way up and did the same with his pants. "I think you can get it the rest of the way," she said.

"I can't believe you would give up right before the finish line," Joe said, smiling.

"You'd like to think I have a horse in this race, wouldn't you?" Katie said before adding, "You dirty old man."

Now, it was Katie's turn to get dressed. She pulled out a pair of blue jeans, a sweater, and a sexy lace bra and panties. She felt like teasing Joe, so she dressed herself very slowly in front of him. "You can look, but don't touch," she told him.

"You really know how to torture a guy."

# Chapter 6

A little while later, there was a knock on the door just before it swung open, and a middle-aged man stepped inside. He pulled off his hat, revealing short, salt-and-pepper hair. He said, "Hey, Pops. Whose car is that out... oh, sorry. I didn't know you had company."

"Good morning, Michael," Joe said. "This is my new friend, Katie. We sort of ran into each other yesterday."

Michael reached out his hand and said, "Pleased to meet you, Katie. I'm sorry. I'm just not used to Joe having visitors."

"You called him Pops."

"Yeah, well, that is sort of an inside joke."

"It's okay, Michael. She knows."

"She knows? What exactly does she know?"

"Everything."

"Everything? Are you crazy? You would risk your future for the first pretty face that comes along?"

"Do you really think I'm pretty?" Katie asked.

"Of course, you're pretty, but that's not the point."

"Michael, relax," Joe said. "I didn't tell her because she's pretty. I told her because there was an accident, and things became obvious."

"An accident? What kind of accident?"

Katie spoke up and said, "Well, I sort of ran into him with my car during the snowstorm yesterday."

"You hit him with your car? How did that happen? Are you alright, Pops?"

"I will be. My leg is still a bit sore, but it will heal."

"What the hell were you doing on the street in the middle of a snowstorm, Pops?"

"I was checking my mailbox."

"Our mailman doesn't come until the afternoon on Saturdays," Michael said. "You know that."

"I know, but I forgot to check it on Friday."

Michael looked at Katie and said, "I think he has developed memory problems in his old age."

"Don't listen to him, Katie," Joe said. "I was forgetting things long before he was born."

Katie laughed and said, "You two sound like my parents."

"I hope that's a good thing," Joe said.

"It is a good thing," Katie said.

"Don't worry about working today, Pops. It's slow because of the storm, and you need rest."

"Katie has a reservation at the resort. Perhaps you can help get her settled in," Joe said.

"Oh, you must be Katie Knight. We assumed you didn't come because of the weather."

"That would be me, and, in a way, the weather was to blame."

"Did your partner not come along?" Michael asked.

"No. It's just me," Katie said.

"Okay, Katie. Grab your things, and I will get you settled into your room."

"If it's okay with both of you, I'd like to stay here with Joe. I feel responsible for his well-being and want to help him until he is better."

Michael looked at Joe and smiled. "What do you think, Pops? Can you handle being doted over by a pretty lady for another day?"

"I will persevere," Joe said.

Michael looked at Katie and quietly said, "Joe is a good man. Please don't hurt him." He then walked out the door.

"Partner?" Joe asked.

"I recently broke up with my boyfriend."

"I'm sorry to hear that."

"Thanks, but it was for the best," Katie said. "So, tell me, how is Michael related to you? Is he your grandson?"

"Yes. He's my grandson."

"How many children do you have?"

"I had three children with my wife, Marie: two boys and a girl. Michael is my daughter's son. Both my boys are gone, but my daughter is still with me. She lives not far from here. Perhaps you will meet her."

"What about grandchildren?"

"Let's see. I have three grandsons, two granddaughters, seven great-grandchildren, two great-great-grandchildren, and one on the way. Everyone has followed their own path, and only my daughter, her eldest son, and his son live here in Wisconsin."

"Let's talk about you, Katie Knight. Is that your real name?" Joe asked.

"My real name is Katherine Kowalczyk. Not exactly a good news anchor name."

"Didn't you tell me that you are not a news anchor?"

"Don't rub it in," Katie said.

"I'm just saying that you have a nice Polish name. There is nothing wrong with it. In the old days, celebrities were much more concerned that their names sounded simple and American, but there are no genuine American names except for Native Americans. All the others originated somewhere else. Besides, nobody cares what your last name is these days."

"You have a point, but I don't know. Besides, I'm only half Polish. Coincidentally, my mother's side has some Croatian in it, too."

"Really? So, we could be related."

"Everybody's related if you go back far enough."

"So, how far back do you have to go to get to your Croatian ancestors?"

"I'm not sure," Katie said. "Let me think. My mother's father's mother came to America shortly after the war ended. I think it was 1919. I remember she was three at the time, and she came with only her mother. Holy crap, Joe! Not only was she born the same year as you, but she also came to America almost the same way you did."

"Do you know what part of the country she came from?"

"No. I'm afraid not." Katie said. "She died when I was around twelve. I was never concerned with my family history at that age. I do remember her telling me that her mother spoke four languages. I remember one of those languages was Hungarian. Perhaps she was born near that country."

"That is very interesting, Katie. If you want to practice being an investigative reporter, you can do research on your own family's history."

"That's a good idea, Joe. I think I'll do that."

"Hey, if you would like to help me, I'll make you breakfast."

"I would love breakfast. What can I do to help?"

"Joe pointed to the closet and said, "There's a tripod inside the closet at the bottom left. Get that for me, please."

Katie opened the closet, removed a tripod from the corner, and handed it to Joe. "Are you still into photography?" she asked.

"Yes. I used to be a professional photographer. I love landscape and wildlife photography the most. One of the reasons I love living here is that there are a lot of photo opportunities nearby. I have many investments, and I don't need to work, but I still make a little extra money selling my photographs, and I really enjoy it."

"That's great, Joe, and I would love to see your photos, but how does this help you make breakfast?"

"I'll show you," he said as he extended the legs part-way and locked them in place. He then stood up and used the tripod as a cane as he hobbled into the kitchen.

"That's pretty ingenious," Katie said.

"When you've lived as long as I have, you learn to work with what you have."

A pan was already on the stove, and Joe turned on the flame. He then removed a package of bacon from the refrigerator and added several pieces to the pan. He found another pan and cracked a few eggs into it, then added a little cream and some salt and pepper. He stirred that up and then flipped over the bacon.

Katie, wanting to help, looked through the cabinets and pulled out a couple of plates and a couple of forks. She found the bread and added a couple of slices to his toaster. When the toast was done, she buttered the pieces and added them to the plates seconds before Joe added the bacon and eggs.

"We make a good team," Joe said as Katie carried the plates to the small table. "Oh, I almost forgot. There's orange juice in the fridge. Sorry, but I don't drink coffee."

"Orange juice is fine," Katie said. She removed it from the refrigerator and poured it into two glasses that she found in the same cabinet as the plates.

After they sat down to eat, Katie said, "Tell me, Joe. What is your real name?"

"Well, I was adopted at a very young age and grew up with what some would consider the very American name of Joseph Young. What you would call my real name is the one my mother gave me before she died. That is Josip Novak. That is the name I use today. As you can imagine, I have needed to change my identity a few times during my life. I couldn't very well be celebrating my eightieth birthday, or hundredth for that matter, looking like this."

"I can imagine that would be a problem," Katie said. "Why did you go back to your original name? Might that not become an issue for you?"

"I wanted to honor my parents," Joe said. "Josip was also my father's name. I didn't think it would be an issue because Josip Novak only existed on paper in 1916. I went to school as Joseph Young."

"How do you know what name your mother chose for you if she died when you were born?" Katie asked.

"I'll show you," Joe said, getting up from the table and limping across the room. He opened the bottom drawer of his nightstand, pulled out a scrapbook, and returned to the kitchen table. He opened it to the first page and handed it to Katie.

Katie opened the book and saw many pages of plastic protective sleeves with various pieces of memorabilia. The first page had an old, yellowed note written in another language. "Did your mother write this?" she asked.

"Yes. It asks that I be looked after, and it specifies the names she wanted if I were a boy or a girl, as well as why she picked those names. She says Josip was my father's name."

"Do you speak the Croatian language?"

"No. I never had a need to learn it. My mother told me what the letter said in a nutshell, and later, I found someone who translated it word for word for me. The translation is on the next page."

Katie flipped the page and saw another letter on yellowed paper. This one was written in English. Katie read the letter and said, "It seems your real mother loved you before she even met you."

"Yes, I believe she did. I only wish she had lived long enough to get to know me."

Katie reached over and squeezed Joe's hand. "I'm sure she's looking down and smiling at you. When did you learn that you were adopted?"

"I don't know, exactly. My parents never tried to hide the truth from me. I think I understood what it meant to be adopted at around six or seven years old."

"Were your adoptive parents good to you?"

"Yes. Both of my parents loved me. They didn't treat me any differently than they treated their other kids. I was lucky," Joe said. "Do you still want to help me learn where I came from?"

"Of course. I would love to help," Katie said.

"You can start by taking a picture of that letter. Maybe you can find out something from it."

Katie grabbed her phone and took a picture of the letter. She then started flipping through the book before Joe reached over and took it from her. "There's nothing else in there that would help you," he said before returning the book to the drawer from which he had taken it.

When he returned to the kitchen, Katie said, "I'm sorry. I didn't mean to be nosey."

"You're a reporter. It's in your nature to be nosey. You have nothing to be sorry for. I'm just not ready to share my whole life yet."

When they finished breakfast, Katie offered to clean the kitchen. When she finished, they sat down on the sofa together. "I'm sorry I don't have a television," Joe said.

"Don't be sorry," Katie said. "I came here to get away from television, among other things."

"I was thinking," Joe said. "How are you going to drive home with a broken windshield?"

"Shit! I forgot all about that," Katie said as she got up and went outside to look at it. She brushed the snow away and saw a large, spiderweb-like crack in the center of the glass.

Joe got up, stood at the door, and watched while Katie examined the window. She looked back at Joe and said, "I can't drive it like this. I will surely get a ticket if I try."

"I guess we'll be going to the resort after all," Joe said. "You can use the phone there. Come back inside and pack your stuff."

Katie returned to the cabin and said, "I hate to leave you, Joe. I wanted to help you as long as I could."

"You're not leaving me. I'm going with you. Someone needs to show you the way. Your GPS is obviously not up to the task."

"Thank you, Joe," Katie said before packing what she took from her suitcase. She zipped it up, put on her coat, and pulled the suitcase out the door with Joe following behind.

Katie opened the trunk, and Joe picked up her suitcase and put it inside. She noticed he wasn't using his tripod as a cane and said, "Where's your tripod?"

"My leg is feeling a bit better, and I didn't feel like dragging that thing along," Joe said.

Katie looked at him, shook her head, and said, "Your secret is safe with me, Joe, because if I told anyone, people would think I was crazy."

"Maybe you are," Joe said as he got into the passenger seat.

Katie got in, buckled up, and said with a smile, "If I were sane, would I still be here?"

"I would guess not," Joe said.

Katie backed up until she reached the end of the driveway, stopped, and asked, "Which way do I go?"

"Go left, the way you came from, and then turn right on the first street you come to."

Katie followed his directions and drove slowly because her visibility was limited. There were also several inches of snow on the road, which made driving even more difficult. When she reached the main road, she said, "This was the road I was on, and that damned GPS made me turn."

"Sometimes technology is not our friend," Joe said.

They drove for less than a quarter of a mile when the Three Eagles Ski Resort entrance appeared. "I can't believe how close this is. I could have walked here," Katie said.

"In a snowstorm?" Joe asked.

"Well, maybe not," Katie admitted.

***

She parked the car and followed Joe inside. Michael was behind the desk, as well as a young man who looked to be around Joe's age, or his apparent age, anyway. "Pops," Michael said. "I thought you were going to stay home and rest."

"I'm feeling better, and Katie needs to use the phone, so I figured she should use her room."

"Of course," Michael said. He found the correct key and handed it to her. "It's room 109. Can you show her where it is, Pops?"

"Right this way, my dear," Joe said.

As they started to leave, the young man had just finished with a guest, looked up, and said, "Grandpa, er, I mean, Joe. I thought you weren't coming in today."

"It's okay, Eric. She knows. This is Katie. Katie, this is my great-grandson, Eric."

The two of them shook hands, and Joe said, "How's Rachael doing?"

"Okay, I guess," he said. "You know, being eight months pregnant is hard. She can never get comfortable."

"Women definitely get the hard part when it comes to having children," Joe said. "The only thing you can do is be there when she needs you, and don't take it personally when she yells at you."

"I'll keep that in mind, Grandpa."

Katie's room was beautiful. There was an old-fashioned, four-post king-size bed in the middle of the room with a sofa and a couple of chairs on either side of a sliding glass door that overlooked the ski slopes. There was a sitting area outside, but it was too cold to sit outside. Katie assumed it was mostly for smokers or crazy people who liked the cold.

"Do you like your room?" Joe asked.

"I love it," Katie said. "I only wish I had more time to enjoy it."

"There is a phone next to the bed. You can call about your windshield and anyone else you need to talk to. I'll be at the front desk if you need me."

"I'm curious, Joe. Why is this place called Three Eagles Ski Resort?"

"Because it's a ski resort," Joe said, laughing.

Katie shook her head and said, "You're a funny guy, Joe, but really, why 'Three Eagles'?"

"A long time ago, before I was born, a female Bald Eagle had a nest at the top of the hill. She had two male companions who both helped her raise her two eaglets. Those three eagles returned three years in a row to the same nest to raise new eaglets."

"That's quite a story. Is it true?"

"People around here think so," Joe said. "I'll leave you alone so you can make your phone calls."

"Thank you so much, Joe."

Katie called her insurance company and reported that a large bird hit her car. She felt bad about lying, but she couldn't tell them she hit a man who was fine now, especially one who did not want attention. The insurance company put her in touch with a glass company that could not get out to her until two o'clock the next day.

She then called her boss, told him the situation, and said she would probably not be able to make it back in time for work on Monday. He wasn't happy about it, but if she was being honest with herself, she didn't care too much.

Next, she called her mother. She told her a half-truth. She said she hit a man with her car and has been helping him recover, but she implied his injuries were minor.

"Is he single?" her mother asked.

"Mom, I didn't come here to find a man."

"He is single, isn't he? Is he good-looking?"

"Mom, stop! I just called to let you know what's happening. I've got to go."

"Okay, Dear, but I want to hear all about him when you get home."

"Mom, please. He's just a guy who I will probably never see again after tomorrow."

"Tomorrow? You mean you are staying another night with him?"

"Bye, Mom. I have to go."

# Chapter 7

Joe limped back to the front desk and met Michael and Eric there. Eric was busy with a guest. When he finished, he said, "I noticed you have a little bit of a limp, Grandpa. What happened?"

"Just a little car accident," Joe said.

"But you don't have a car, Grandpa."

"She does," Joe said, pointing toward Katie's room.

"Oh, I see," Eric said. "You know, there are easier ways to meet women."

"I'll try to remember that."

"So, what do you think of her, Pops?" Michael asked.

"Katie? She's okay."

"Just, okay? You told her your secret after one day. She better be more than okay."

"I didn't have much choice. She saw me get better. She's a reporter. She said she would investigate me if I didn't tell her."

"A reporter? All the more reason to keep your mouth shut," Michael said. "I think you wanted to tell her. I think you see something special in her."

"Nonsense. I mean, I like her, and she's attractive, but so are a lot of women."

"You've got to stop living like this, Pops. You can't keep pushing women away. When was the last time you had a serious relationship? You haven't. Not since Grandma died, and that was over twenty years ago. Now you live like a hermit in that cabin of yours."

"I do not live like a hermit. You don't know what you are talking about."

"Really, Pops? I understand that Grandma was the love of your life. I get that. You think having a meaningful relationship will somehow diminish what you two had together. It won't. You can love more than one person."

"Yes, but the love of a lifetime only comes along once," Joe said.

"How would you know that, Pops? You've never given love a chance. You have been given this wonderful gift of youth, and you squander it."

Just then, Katie walked up to the counter, and the conversation stopped. "Did I interrupt something?" she asked.

"We were just discussing relationships," Joe said. "Perhaps you have some advice you would like to share."

"I'm the wrong person to ask for relationship advice. I can tell you from experience what not to do. That's about it."

"So, are you planning on hitting the slopes while you are here?" Joe asked.

"I'm really not much of a skier. Perhaps you could show me the ropes if your leg is up to it."

"I don't think it is healed enough yet. Perhaps we can go out tomorrow morning if you are still here."

"I can't get the window fixed until tomorrow afternoon."

"Okay, great. Tomorrow it is. Right now, I bet you are getting hungry for lunch. We have a fantastic restaurant here at the resort. Can I take you there?"

"That sounds wonderful, Joe. I am feeling a bit hungry," Katie said.

Joe whispered something to Eric before coming around to meet Katie. He held out his arm, which Katie took, and led her to the restaurant. When they arrived, the hostess sat them at a small table near the window. A few minutes later, Eric met them at the table with two glasses and a bottle of champagne. He poured the champagne and said, "Hello, ma'am. Hello, sir. I will be your waiter this afternoon."

Katie laughed and said, "Eric, you're a waiter too?"

"I do a little of everything around here, Miss Katie. Give me a minute. I have one more thing for you." He returned with a cupcake that had one burning candle stuck in it. He set it in front of Katie as several of the restaurant staff arrived at the table. They all sang Happy Birthday to her.

When they finished, Katie smiled and said, "That was great. Thank you all so much."

She blew out the candle, and everyone clapped before returning to their duties. Katie looked at Joe and said, "I assume you had something to do with this."

"Maybe a little."

Katie leaned over and kissed him on the cheek. "That was very nice of you."

"Happy birthday, old lady," he said.

"Thank you, old man."

Katie opened her menu, and Joe said, "The prime rib is awesome here."

"Okay then," she said. "I'll get the prime rib."

"You can't," Joe said. "They only serve it for dinner."

Katie playfully slapped Joe with her menu and said, "Thanks. You've been a great help."

"Seriously, though, I like the mushroom Swiss burger for lunch."

"Okay, that sounds tasty."

"Unfortunately, they only have that on Saturday."

Katie slapped him with her menu again and said, "Will you stop?"

Eric returned and asked if they had decided what they wanted. Katie said, "I'll have the mushroom Swiss burger."

"I'm sorry, Miss Katie," Eric said. "That's only available on Saturday."

Joe started laughing, and Katie slapped him with her hand this time. "Did you put him up to that?"

Eric laughed and said, "I'm sorry, Miss Katie. I overheard you two and couldn't resist. I will put you down for a mushroom Swiss burger."

"I can tell you two are related," Katie said.

Joe told Eric he would have the same thing, and when Eric left, he said, "So, I want to hear more about you. How did you end up as a reporter, or news personality, or whatever you called it?"

"I grew up in a small, rinky-dink Wisconsin town on the Mississippi. We were about as far from anything interesting as one could get. I wanted out, so I went to college in Milwaukee. When I graduated, I got a job at a Milwaukee television station. I started as an intern, but I gradually became an on-air personality. The problem is, I can't get the opportunity to do real stories."

"Why do you think what you do is not real?" Joe asked.

"It's real, I guess, but it's not important. I mean, who cares about the city's biggest cookie or the bar that pretends to be an import company?"

"Those both sound interesting," Joe said. "Do you know why I don't have a television? I did several years ago, and mostly only watched the news on it. After a while, I realized that almost all the news was bad, and most of that bad news was unnecessary to know. Does anyone really need to know about the dictator on the other side of the world or the murder that happened on the other side of town? The kind of stories you do are the only stories worth watching. You think reporting the bad news will somehow make you more important, but I disagree. You, Katherine Kowalczyk, singlehandedly keep your news station from totally sucking."

Katie laughed and said, "That was a great speech, Joe, but reporting the bad news pays better."

"You should do what you feel passionate about. Never put money above passion. You will regret it."

"Unfortunately, Joe, in the real world, money is important."

"Money is important up to a point. You only need enough money to survive comfortably, and you can make that money doing what you are passionate about."

"I'm sorry, Joe, but I'm not passionate about human interest stories. I need something that will challenge me mentally."

"Well then, perhaps an investigative reporter position will be right for you. If that is the case, I hope you get what you want."

"Thank you, Joe. I hope so, too."

"What about friends?" Joe asked. "What do you do for fun?"

"My best friend still lives in my hometown. I make it back there three or four times a year. I have a couple of friends from work, and sometimes we go out, but I mostly hang out at my apartment when I'm not working. I'm probably a bit of a hermit like you."

"I'm not a hermit. Why does everyone keep saying that?"

"Okay, Mr. Sociable. When did you last leave your cabin to do something fun with another human being?"

"Well, I don't know. It wasn't that long ago."

"Really? What did you do? Who were you with?"

Joe stumbled on his words. "Uh, I don't know. I can't remember."

"You must have had a really good time if you can't remember," Katie said.

"Okay, you win," Joe said. "Let's just say I like spending time at home."

Just then, Eric arrived with their burgers. He put the plates down and said, "I hope you enjoy, Miss Katie."

"That was fast. Thanks so much, Eric," Katie said before he walked away.

Katie took a bite of her burger and said, "Mmmm. This is good."

"Stick with me, kid, and you can't go wrong," Joe said.

"You can probably eat like this every day, and it doesn't bother you," Katie said.

"I wish," Joe said. "I need to watch my diet just like you."

"That's surprising after what I have seen you do."

"I'm lucky, in a way, because I can tell what nutrients my body lacks."

"You are lucky in more than one way, but can't all people do that? I mean, If I crave something salty, doesn't that mean I need more salt?"

"It is supposed to work that way, but the unconscious mind can be fooled. For example, have you ever craved a jelly donut?"

"Who hasn't?" Katie asked.

"When that happens, do you think your body is deficient in jelly donuts?"

"Well, since you put it that way, I suppose not."

"It is your unconscious mind mistaking want for need. Essentially, it is an addiction like heroin."

"Are you saying sugar is as addictive as heroin?"

"Of course not. It's more addictive. I try to avoid sugar and eat healthy food as much as possible. It is how I am able to stay this good-looking." Katie had just taken a bite of her burger, but spat it out when she laughed. "I'm sorry, but you really know how to make a girl laugh."

"You mean you don't find me attractive?" Joe asked.

"I think you are quite handsome, Joe, but you already knew that."

"I find you quite attractive as well, Katie."

There was an awkward moment of silence, and then Katie said, "I'm really glad I ran into you. I mean, I'm not glad I ran into you. I'm sorry I ran into you. I guess what I am trying to say is I'm glad we met."

"I know what you mean, Katie, and I'm glad we met, too."

When they finished lunch, they returned to the front desk, and Joe said, "I know something you might like to do. Grab your coat and meet me out front in five minutes." He walked behind the counter, picked up a set of keys, and disappeared through a door in the back.

The thought of a surprise excited Katie. She thought it foolish but couldn't help feeling like a child on Christmas morning. She quickly retrieved her coat and waited outside for Joe.

\*\*\*

Joe showed up on a snowmobile a few minutes later. He handed Katie a helmet and a pair of gloves. He said, "Put these on and get on."

Katie put on the helmet and gloves, climbed onto the snowmobile, and put her arms around Joe's waist. "I've never been on a snowmobile before," she shouted.

"You're kidding!" Joe said. "I thought you were a Wisconsin girl."

"I have no excuse," Katie said.

They were soon on a trail that wound through the woods as it gradually gained altitude. They passed a couple on another snowmobile going in the opposite direction. Katie could see the trail was well-worn with tracks and assumed this was a popular place for snowmobiles. "We rent snowmobiles at the resort," Joe said. "Some people like it better than skiing."

As the next turn came up, Joe hit the accelerator, and Katie screamed. "Slow down! Slow down!" she said. "You're going to give me a heart attack."

Joe slowed the snowmobile and laughed. "I think you've been living in the city too long."

They wound their way up the trail until it leveled out. Joe pulled over to the side and stopped. He stepped off and held out his hand. Katie grabbed it and got off. Without letting go, Joe said. "Come with me," and led Katie through a group of trees to a clearing. From there, they could look down on the ski resort from over a mile away.

"It's beautiful," Katie said.

"Our mountains here are nowhere near as high as those in Colorado, but I wouldn't trade this view for the world."

"I can see where you would get your inspiration for your photography."

"You should see it in the fall," Joe said.

"I would love that. Are you inviting me back?" Katie asked.

"I would be happy to see you anytime, Katie. Just tell me when you are coming so I can avoid checking my mail that day."

Joe laughed, and Katie slapped him on the arm. He winced in pain, and Katie said. "Oh, my God! I'm sorry! I thought your arm was better."

Joe laughed and said, "I got you!"

She tried slapping him again, but Joe jumped back, and she missed. She chased him through the woods, and when they almost reached the snowmobile, she stopped and said, "Hey! Your limp is gone."

Joe looked down, felt his leg, and said, "What do you know? It's better."

"Well, I guess you don't need me anymore," Katie said.

"There are different kinds of needs," Joe said. He studied her face momentarily and asked, "What is it that you need, Katie?"

Katie hesitated momentarily, then walked toward the snowmobile and got on the back. "I think we should head back."

"Did I say something wrong?"

"No. You've been wonderful. It's me. I'm a mess. I don't know what I need. I don't know what I want. I don't know where my life is going. I certainly don't want to drag you down with me."

"You need time to think," Joe said as he got on the snowmobile. "I'll take you back, and if you want to talk, I'll be here."

They drove back to the resort, and Katie said she wanted to be alone to rest, so they said their goodbyes and agreed to meet the following morning.

# Chapter 8

Katie checked her phone when she got back to her room. She had a signal, but it was weak. She dialed Ashley's number.

"Hi, Katie," Ashley said. "How goes your weekend getaway?"

"It certainly is not what I expected," Katie said.

"Is that good or bad?"

"I don't know," Katie said. "I hit a man with my car during the snowstorm on the way up here."

"Oh, my God! Is he okay?"

"He's okay now, but I can't get my windshield fixed until tomorrow afternoon."

"Your windshield? How hard did you hit him? How is he okay?"

"It turns out he's quite resilient."

"Sounds like my kind of man. Is he cute?"

"Stop. Now you sound like my mother."

"You talked to your mother about him? He must be special."

"He is special but not in that way," Katie said. "I just felt bad that I hit him, so I stayed with him to ensure he was okay."

"Why didn't you get him medical attention?" Ashley asked.

'It was in the middle of a snowstorm. I had no cell signal, and he doesn't have a phone."

"He doesn't have a phone? He must be one of those rugged, outdoor types. So, you spent the night with him?"

"Yes, but I didn't sleep with him if that's what you're getting at," Katie said.

"Well, there's always tonight."

"No, there isn't. I told him I had to rest and wanted to be alone."

"Are you crazy?" Ashley asked. "Do you sabotage relationships on purpose?"

"What are you talking about? I didn't sabotage Brad."

"Listen," Ashley said. "I was never a Brad fan, and I think you are better off without him, but that's not the point. Are you sure you weren't looking for a reason to end it? The same goes for Alan and that other guy. What was his name?"

"Bob."

"Bob. Right. What about Bob?" Ashley said and laughed.

"Very funny, Ashley. You should know I didn't sabotage any of those relationships. I just happen to be very particular, and none of those men were right for me."

"We all have flaws, Katie. The perfect man is the one you can put up with. My husband has plenty of flaws and annoys the crap out of me sometimes, but he loves me and treats me like a princess."

"So, how did you know John was the right man for you?"

"When you find the right one, you just know."

"Yeah. That's what my mom said."

"Your mom is right. By the way, did you hear that David is moving up to corporate, and Stephen will take his place as anchor?"

"Really? That means that there will be an open position for an investigative reporter. Do you know anything about that?"

"No, but I imagine it would go to you or Kevin. It's too bad you won't be in tomorrow. You need to show them . . ."

Just then, the phone went dead. Katie looked and saw she lost the signal. She thought about calling Ashley back on the hotel phone, but there was no point. She sat on the bed and thought about her situation. She thought about what Joe had said. Would this new job make her happy? Would she enjoy hard news stories? She was sitting on one right here. She had to think.

She opened her laptop and connected it to the resort's Wi-Fi. She looked up "Croatian Americans Wisconsin" and found a Croatian American club in Milwaukee. She went to their website and found an email address. She then connected her phone to her laptop, downloaded the photo of the letter from Joe's mother, and attached it to an email. She asked for help determining where the woman who wrote the letter was from. She signed it using her real name, sent the email, closed her laptop, and sat back to think.

Thirty minutes later, the sound of an email arriving awakened her. She had dozed off. She was more tired than she realized. She opened her laptop and read the email. It was from a woman named Martina Pavlovic. "Dear Ms. Kowalczyk. Thank you for your email. Judging by the writing and the last name of Novak, the woman who wrote the letter probably came from the northwestern part of the country, near where the border of Slovenia and

Hungary meet. I know someone who comes from that area and will contact her about it to see if she knows anything more."

Katie wrote back, "Thank you so much. Please also ask her if she has heard any stories of very long-lived people in the area."

She searched the internet for stories of Croatian people with very long lives. She tried every search term she could think of, but nothing relevant came up. She did learn that women live four years longer than men, which she found a bit ironic. After a while, she felt hungry and realized it was almost six, so she put her laptop away and headed to the restaurant.

When she arrived, she was seated right away near the window, like last time. It was already almost dark, but the slopes were lit up, and she could see a few skiers out there, but not nearly as many as at lunchtime. The restaurant was also relatively empty. Sunday night was probably not a typically busy time of the week.

A woman came to her table to take her order, and Katie asked, "Is Eric here?"

"I'm sorry, but Eric comes in early on the weekends. He's gone home already."

"What about Joe?"

"I think he's gone too. At least I haven't seen him in a while."

"That's okay," Katie said. "Do you have the prime rib tonight?"

"Oh, that's a great choice. Would you like something to drink?"

"A Coke, please," she said. She then thought about what Joe said about addiction and changed it to an unsweetened iced tea.

After dinner, Katie wandered up to the front desk. There was a woman behind the counter whom she didn't recognize. She said, "Is Joe still here?"

"No, I'm sorry," the woman said. "He went home a little while ago."

"Thank you," Katie said and walked to the front door. A light snow was coming down, and Katie briefly considered walking to his cabin. Was she crazy? Did she really want to risk getting lost and freezing to death? She banished the thought from her mind and returned to her room.

She opened her laptop and read an email that was waiting for her. "Hello, Ms. Kowalczyk. My contact agrees that she probably came from the country's northwestern part and personally knows several Novaks in the area. She was intrigued by your question about long-lived people. She has heard stories of a small settlement near a town called Dekanovec. According to legend, a Healer is born once or twice a century. This Healer never ages and passes his knowledge on to the next Healer. The Healers can be killed, but they never die of old age. Of course, it's just a legend."

Katie closed her laptop and put on her coat and gloves. She tucked her laptop under her arm and went to the front desk. "Can anyone drive me to Joe's house?" she asked.

The woman gave her an awkward look and said, "Joe is not a big fan of visitors, if you know what I mean."

"He'll want to see me," Katie said.

"Unfortunately, there is nobody available at this time."

"That's okay," Katie said.

She returned to her room, sat on the bed, and thought awhile. Was she crazy? She would stay in her room and go to bed early if she were smart.

She got up, put her coat on, grabbed her laptop, and went outside. She walked to her car, hesitated for a moment, then opened the door and got in.

Driving with a cracked window at night while it was snowing was not easy, but Katie made it back to Joe's cabin. She grabbed her laptop and pounded on his door.

The door opened, and a surprised Joe said, "Katie! What are you doing here?"

"Can I come in?"

"Of course," Joe said as he stepped aside to let her in.

She put her laptop down and took off her gloves. She then put her hands on Joe's face and kissed him. "I'm sorry. I know what I need now," She kissed him again.

The kissing became passionate, and Katie removed her coat and unbuttoned Joe's shirt. She took it off and examined his body. It was flawless.

She let Joe unbutton her shirt and take it off. She reached back to unbutton her bra, but Joe stopped her. "No. Let me do it." When her bra was off, Joe looked at her and said, "You are so beautiful."

He picked her up and placed her gently on the bed. They made love for hours before falling asleep together.

***

Katie awoke the next morning to an empty bed. She looked up and saw Joe in front of the stove. He noticed she was awake and said, "Good morning, Sunshine. I hope you like French toast."

"I love it," she said as she sat up and looked for her clothes. She put them on and sat down at the small dining room table.

Joe placed a plate of French toast in front of her and another plate across from her. He placed silverware on the table along with butter and maple syrup. He sat down and said, "Bon appétit."

Katie put a little butter and syrup on her French toast, took a bite, and said, "This is delicious. Thank you, Joe, but you didn't have to go through the trouble."

"No trouble at all. I would have made it for myself if you weren't here. Somehow, your presence makes it so much better."

"I came here last night to show you something."

"Really?" Joe said. "I thought you might have come for a different reason."

"Well, I did come here because I wanted to see you, but I also wanted to show you what I found."

"What you found? Do you mean about the letter?"

"Yes, I know where your mother was from, and there are rumors of more people like you."

Joe put his fork down and asked, "Are you serious?"

"Yes. I'll show you the email."

"Let's finish our breakfast first," Joe said. "I've waited this long. A few more minutes won't hurt."

When they finished eating, Katie put her laptop on the table and opened her email program. She turned the screen toward Joe so he could read the message. "Healer," he said. "What do you think she means by Healer? I'm not a Healer."

"I don't know. Maybe knowing how your own body works helps you to know how it works in other people."

"That is true to a certain extent," Joe said, "but it sounds like these people were born to be Healers, like they had a gift for healing other people. I don't feel that way. Can you ask her how those people were able to heal others?"

"I can, but not from here. I have no internet here."

"Okay," Joe said. "Let's go back to your room where there's internet."

43

They worked together cleaning the kitchen. When they finished, they put their coats on and drove back to the resort. When they arrived, Michael was at the front counter and said, "Good morning, Pops. Good morning, Katie. Are you keeping the old man out of trouble?"

Katie laughed and said, "Short of running him over with my car, I don't know how that's possible."

Once they were back in Katie's room, she opened her laptop and responded to the email again. This time, she asked the woman if she could learn more about the Healers, specifically how they healed people. She also asked if there might be one alive today. She put the laptop away and sat on the bed when she finished.

Joe sat beside her, kissed her, and said, "Thank you for looking into that for me. I suddenly feel a connection to the parents I never knew."

Katie kissed him and said, "Anything for you, Joe." They kissed some more, and then Katie stood up and led Joe to the shower. They washed each other thoroughly and made love with the warm water flowing over them.

They both felt cold when they got out of the shower, so they got in bed under the covers and held each other. "I know I said I would take you skiing today, so if you want, we can go out into the cold, or we can stay here in the warmth together."

"I really didn't care much about skiing anyway," Katie said. "Now, shut up and kiss me."

# Chapter 9

They lay in bed together until around noon and then got dressed and had lunch together. When they returned to Katie's room, she opened her laptop and checked her email. There was a reply from the Croatian woman, "In response to your question, the Healer is supposed to be able to cure people of any ailment simply by touching them. Of course, you understand that this is merely a legend. My contact would like to know if you know someone like that."

Joe was reading over Katie's shoulder and said, "How is that possible? I can't heal other people. Maybe we are barking up the wrong tree here. Maybe a legend is just a legend."

"No. Too many pieces fit together," Katie said. "Are you sure you can't heal other people? Have you tried?"

"Well, no, but you would think I would know what I can and can't do after over a hundred years."

"Perhaps, but why don't you try to heal me?"

"There's nothing to heal. You're fine."

"How do you know? If you can read your own body, maybe you can read mine. Just try," Katie said and held out her hands.

Joe took her hands in his, closed his eyes, and concentrated. "Nothing," he said after about a minute of trying. "I can't even feel what's going on inside your body, much less fix it."

"Well, it was worth a shot," she said. "Maybe there is a trick to it that you haven't figured out yet."

"It's too bad I didn't come with a manual."

"You wouldn't read it anyway. You're a man," Katie said and smiled. She sensed his disappointment and wanted to cheer him up.

"I can't argue with you there," Joe said before getting up to look out the window. He wanted to think.

Katie replied to the email and said, "No, I don't know anyone with that kind of ability."

The room phone rang to inform Katie that the auto glass guy was there to replace her window. She and Joe met him in the parking lot, and while he was working, Katie told Joe, "I need to go back home when he finishes the window.

An investigative reporter position has opened up at the station, and they are considering me for the job. Showing up late today will look better than not showing up at all."

"I understand," Joe said. "You need to do what is important for you."

"It's my career. It is important to me, but that doesn't mean you are not. Why don't you come with me? You can stay with me until Saturday, and then we can come back here."

"That is a tempting offer, Katie, but then what? You have your life and career in Milwaukee, and mine is here. I don't see that changing anytime soon."

"Are you always so analytical?" Katie asked somewhat angrily. "I need to go back to my room and pack. I'll say goodbye to you before I leave." She quickly walked back to her room, leaving Joe standing in the parking lot.

Joe walked to the front counter, where Michael and Eric were standing. Eric said, "Miss Katie looked angry. What happened?"

"She asked me to go home with her, and I said no."

Michael looked at Joe and said, "Pops, I love you, but sometimes it seems you haven't learned anything in the last hundred years. You have a chance at real love here with a lovely woman that you clearly care about, but you are willing to let her slip through your fingers for what? Yes, she is not Grandma, but she makes you happy. What is the purpose of life if it is not to be happy?"

"It's complicated," Joe said.

"Then uncomplicate it or embrace the complication. There is nothing wrong with complications. It's better than boring."

"I suppose you're right, Michael. What's the worst that can happen?"

"What are you waiting for? Go get her."

Joe walked quickly to Katie's room and met her as she pulled her suitcase out the door. They stopped and looked at each other for a moment, and Joe said, "I'm sorry, Katie. I was foolish to say no to you. I have always been an optimistic person, but suddenly, I adopted a pessimistic attitude. That's not me. I have gotten so used to being comfortable that the thought of change scares me, but Michael pointed out that complicated is better than boring, and he's right. I want to go with you if you will still have me. I want you to complicate my life."

Katie let go of her suitcase and kissed Joe. They kissed for several seconds until they both became aware of a couple that couldn't get by because they were blocking the hallway. They stepped aside, a little embarrassed, and Joe said, "Sorry, but this place has a way of igniting passion in people."

Katie laughed and said, "That's one way to promote the resort."

"Follow me," Joe said. "I want to pick up a few things before we go."

He led her past the reception desk and into the office. Two desks sat on the right side of the room, with a small space between them. The closest desk had a desktop computer with two monitors and a pile of manilla folders stacked on the side. In the center was a large desk calendar with many notes scribbled on it. The far desk was relatively clean. A laptop sat on the desk, along with a notepad, a small basket with pens in it, and a photo of an old lady at the far corner.

In front of the far desk stood three storage cabinets. Joe opened the far cabinet. It was filled with cameras and camera accessories. Some cameras were newer digital cameras, and others were very old, perhaps from the thirties or even earlier, Katie thought. There were also a few movie cameras from various eras.

Joe took out what looked like a small black box and said, "This was my first camera. My mother bought it for me when I turned ten. It was shortly after my dad died, when I discovered that I was different from other people. I think she felt like I was in a rut and figured I needed something to get me out of it. It worked. I loved this little camera."

"Not so little by today's standard," Katie said.

"No, but in 1926 it was considered small."

He pulled out another camera. This one looked closer to what Katie considered a real camera. Joe opened it so the lens popped out, revealing a bellows-type camera. "I took this one to war with me."

"Do you have photos from that time?"

Joe pointed at a few photo albums at the top of the cabinet, "The Army didn't get everything," he said.

Katie pulled down one of the albums and turned to the first page. It was an eight-by-ten photo of several soldiers standing in front of a tank, smiling. The next few pages were similar. All were photos of men standing in front of their equipment. Then, there was a photo of several burned-out vehicles and what looked like a charred corpse. She quickly flipped the page and saw a truck loaded with dozens of bodies. She slammed the book shut and said, "These are horrible. I can't imagine what you went through."

"My job was to raise morale by showing photos of happy Americans or unhappy Germans. Many of those photos would have been buried or destroyed if I gave them to the Army."

"I always thought it was the Nazis that were good at propaganda."

"Everybody lies during a war," Joe said.

"Those photos are important for history. You should publish a book or donate them to a museum."

"I thought about donating them," Joe said. "I wanted to wait until there was no reason to censor them. Perhaps now is a good time."

Katie handed Joe the book, and he put it back on the shelf. He then reached in and took out a newer digital camera and a telephoto lens. He placed them in a camera bag that he picked up from the bottom shelf. He closed the doors and said, "I got what I need here. We just need to pick up some clothes at my place, and then we can go."

It's nice that Michael gives you a place to store your stuff. Do you use that desk there, too," she said, pointing to the desk with the laptop on it.

I only use the desk when I have photos to edit. As far as Michael letting me use this space, well, technically, this resort belongs to me. My wife and I bought it about 40 years ago. Several years ago, I put it in my daughter's name when I 'died' and was 'reborn' as Michael's son. She will pass it to me when she dies, and if I die first, then Eric will get 51 percent, and the rest will be split up amongst the great-grandkids."

"Why give 51 percent to Eric?" Katie asked.

"Because Eric is here, and I trust him to keep this place in the family."

"How were you able to change your identity like that?"

"It took me a while to learn the ropes, but you can get almost anything in this country for a price."

"Does it feel weird being the brother of your great-grandson?" Katie asked.

"A little, but I keep a low profile, so it's never an issue."

"Well, we should probably get your clothes and hit the road," Katie said. "I have a boss to impress, and I can't do it from here."

They went back to Joe's cabin, packed a few of his things, and then hit the road. The sun was shining, and the streets were clear, except for an occasional patch of ice. A classic rock station was playing on the radio, but Katie turned the volume most of the way down and said, "So tell me, Joe, what was it like growing up in the twenties?"

"It was very different than these twenties. For one thing, it was hot in the summer."

"How is that different than summers today?" Katie asked.

"Try to imagine living in a small apartment with six people and no air conditioning."

"I didn't think about that. I bet only the super-rich had air conditioners back then."

"I didn't even know air conditioners existed before I was in my teens."

"Did you meet your wife when you were young?"

"I was eighteen. After I finished high school, I enrolled in a photography school. It's still around today, but it was very small back then. They would sometimes bring in people to pose for us so we could practice portrait photography. One day, Marie came in to pose for me, and it was love at first sight. Her family was somewhat wealthy, and she was much more cultured than I was. Her father initially disapproved of our relationship, but her mother liked me, and eventually, her father came around, too."

"Did Marie work too?"

"Oh, yes. After the war, I became somewhat successful as a freelance photographer. Several big magazines printed my photographs. I also sold prints at art shows and eventually opened my own gallery. Marie helped me every step of the way. She developed film, printed photographs, talked to clients, and helped with bookkeeping. She even learned the art of picture framing. I don't think I would have been successful without her."

"You really loved her, didn't you?"

"With every fiber of my being."

There was a moment of silence, and then Joe said, "If that Croatian woman is right, I might have been able to save her. Maybe I could have even kept her young."

"You can't beat yourself up over something you could not have known. Besides, it might not be true, or if it is, it might not be true for you."

"I suppose you may be right," Joe said, "but I hate not knowing for certain."

Katie put her hand on Joe's hand and squeezed but said nothing. What could she say? She wanted to help him but didn't know how.

# Chapter 10

The roads were clear all the way to Milwaukee. They arrived at Katie's apartment just before four-thirty. It was in an old part of town, not too far from downtown. They parked on the street in front of two identical four-story brick buildings. They entered the building on the right, which happened to be at the end of the street. Katie led Joe up the stairs to the third floor. The building had no elevator.

Katie opened the door and said, "I'm sorry, Joe, but I need to hurry up and get ready for work. I'll show you around later." She then disappeared into the bedroom.

Joe closed the door behind him and looked around the apartment. It was old and outdated. It had old-style radiators for heat. Joe liked that it was old. It reminded him of growing up in New York. He guessed the building was almost as old as he was.

The apartment was clean but not entirely tidy. There were a few books and magazines in random places and a few pieces of clothing here and there. Several paintings were hanging on the walls. Most were paintings of chimpanzees, but there was also one painting of a mermaid, which seemed out of place. The kitchen was small but clean and tidier than the rest of the apartment.

The large window in the living room overlooked similar-style apartments across the street. The kitchen had a small window, and that view was different. Joe could see a couple of very tall buildings, one of which was a bank. He wondered why banks needed to be so big. What could all those offices possibly be used for?

After about fifteen minutes, Katie came out of the bedroom wearing a dark red knee-length skirt, a matching shirt with sleeves just past the elbow, and a neckline that showed off just enough cleavage but not too much. The entire outfit was skintight, showing off her perfect curves. "How do I look?" she asked.

Joe looked at her and said, "Wow!"

"That's all I needed to hear. I've got to go," Katie said before quickly kissing Joe and heading to the door.

"Wait a minute," Joe said. "Were you planning on leaving me here?"

"I'm sorry, Joe. I have to work. I will only be a few hours."

"I was hoping that I could see what you do."

Katie thought about it briefly and said, "Okay, what the hell? Just be prepared to be bored."

"I'll prepare myself," Joe said.

They made it to the television station a minute before five. Katie brought Joe through a door marked "Employees Only." It led directly into the newsroom. It was a large room with more than two dozen cubicles. Katie said hello to several people as she and Joe made their way to her desk near the center of the room. Katie sat at her desk and checked her computer for messages.

Ashley saw Katie come in, poked her head around the corner, and said, "Welcome back, Katie. How was your weekend getaway, as if I couldn't guess?"

"It was much needed," Katie said. She then put her hand on Joe's arm and said, "This is Joe. I brought him back with me. They were running a special. Every new guest gets to take home a man."

Ashley smiled, held out her hand, and said, "Pleased to meet you, Joe."

Joe took her hand, kissed it, and said, "The pleasure is all mine."

Ashley giggled and said, "I love to see modern young men with old-world manners. It is so rare these days."

"Joe is definitely one in a million," Katie said.

Ashley looked Joe over and said, "You look great for someone who was hit by a car."

Joe glanced at Katie, surprised that she mentioned it to anyone, then said, "I wouldn't call that thing she drives a car."

Ashley laughed and said, "You have a point. It probably felt like getting hit by a cardboard box."

They both laughed, and Katie said, "Don't make fun of my beautiful car. For your information, he could have been hit by a garbage truck with all that padding he was wearing."

"By the way," Ashley said, "Mr. Martin wants to see you in his office when you get in."

"Is it about the job?" Katie asked.

"I don't know, but it's possible."

"Okay. Do you think you can show Joe around while I'm gone?"

"It would be my pleasure," Ashley said with a smile.

The only office with an actual door was that of the news director, Robert Martin. Katie knocked three times, opened the door, and asked, "Are you free, Mr. Martin?" Most of the news people went by their first names, but Robert Martin was an experienced newsman who naturally commanded a certain amount of respect.

"Come on in, Katie," he said. "Have a seat."

Katie sat down while Martin leaned back in his chair and ran a hand through his thick, white hair. He said, "I know you have been interested in moving into the investigative reporter position, and one has just become available. I've decided to give it to you on a trial basis if you still want it."

"Of course I want it, Mr. Martin. Thank you so much," Katie said. "If you don't mind my asking, I heard Kevin was in the running for the job. Why did you pick me over him?"

"Kevin looks good on television and has a great speaking voice, but I need someone who can dig into a story and find the truth. Quite frankly, I don't think Kevin could find steak at a butcher shop."

Katie tried to hold back a laugh and said, "Well, I appreciate the opportunity, sir. I will try my best not to let you down."

"That's all I can ask. I don't expect perfection on your first day. If you enjoy the work, you will do fine. If you don't, well, I'll keep your old job open as long as I can."

"I appreciate everything you have done for me, Mr. Martin," Katie said. "One more thing. I want to start using my real name."

"That has always been your choice, Miss Kowalczyk. I never believed people cared much about names. What they care about are personality and trust."

"Yes, sir. That's why I decided to go back to my real name. So, do you have an assignment for me?"

"Yes. Go home and relax. I want you to be well rested and ready to go tomorrow."

"Okay, I will do that. Thank you again, sir."

Katie met Joe and Ashley in the newsroom when the meeting was over. Ashley asked, "What happened? Did you get the job?"

"I got the job!" she said excitedly.

"That's fantastic," Ashley said as she hugged her friend.

Joe waited for his turn and hugged Katie, saying, "Congratulations. So, what now?"

"Now, we spend some time together. I have the rest of the evening off."

"You two lovebirds have fun," Ashley said. "I'll see you tomorrow."

When they got into Katie's car, Joe said, "I am very happy for you. I hope this new job is everything you hoped for."

"Thank you, Joe. I hope so, too."

So, what would you like to do now?" Joe asked.

"Honestly, Joe, I just want to pick up a pizza and go home. We can hang out and watch a movie if that's okay with you."

"Sounds like a perfect night," Joe said.

Katie called and ordered a pizza before they left the parking lot. The pizza place was almost on the way home, so they stopped and picked it up. When they arrived at Katie's apartment, she got a couple of plates from the kitchen, and they sat very close together on the couch. They both put their feet on the coffee table, and Katie looked for a movie that they could watch together. She found one that seemed to amuse her, so she put it on.

When Joe realized what movie was playing, he said, "Highlander? Really?"

Katie laughed and said, "There can be only one." She then tried to tickle Joe, but found he wasn't ticklish. On the other hand, Joe found Katie very ticklish and took full advantage of it.

"Wait! Wait! Wait!" Katie said, laughing. "The pizza."

Joe took the plate from her hand and put both plates on the coffee table. He then went back to tickling her. She was on her back laughing, and Joe was on top of her when the tickling stopped and the kissing started. This time, there was no foreplay. It was fast, rough, and passionate. The movie was still playing, and sparks were flying on and off the screen.

When it was over, they sat next to each other on the couch again and finished their pizza. They didn't bother getting dressed. Katie said, "That's the first time I ever ate pizza naked."

"Nude," Joe corrected.

"What?"

"Nude. We ate pizza nude."

"What's the difference?"

"Naked is when your clothes are off. Nude is when you have no clothes on."

"Again, what's the difference?"

"It's more of a feeling. Naked means you're missing something. Nude does not convey the feeling of being without. Do you feel uncomfortable being without clothes right now?"

"Well, no."

"Then you are nude."

"You're pretty smart, Joe."

"I have a lot more useless information up here," Joe said, pointing to his head. "Just ask."

Katie laughed and put her head on his chest.

"That was also the first time I ate pizza nude," Joe said. "So, I guess that was our first first."

"I hope we have many firsts together," Katie said.

Joe turned off the television and said, "I was thinking. Before it gets too late, do you think you can contact that Croatian woman and ask if we could speak with her contact directly? Assuming she is local, that is."

"Of course, Joe," Katie said. "Do you think you can learn something useful from her?"

"I don't know. I hope so."

Katie got her laptop and brought it back to the sofa. She opened it and typed out an email. After she sent the email, she closed the laptop, set it down next to her, and said, "That was the first time I sent an email while nude."

"Let's see what else we can do while nude," Joe said before leaning over to kiss Katie.

# Chapter 11

Katie's alarm went off at seven-thirty. She had fallen asleep with her head on Joe's chest. She had to climb on top of him to reach the alarm. "I see you're already up," she said to Joe.

"It is morning," Joe said. "How late were we up last night?"

"Too late," Katie said. "I've got to get up. It's a big day for me today."

They both got out of bed and took a shower together. When they finished, Katie got her laptop, sat on the edge of the bed, and checked her email. There was a message from the Croatian woman. She said her contact lived in the area and was eager to meet her. She included the woman's name, address, and phone number in the message. Joe was reading over her shoulder and asked, "Can we see her today?"

"Yes, but it will have to be this evening."

Joe nodded, and Katie replied, saying they would call her after work.

Katie put her computer away and then sat at the small dressing table in her bedroom to put her makeup on. While she was doing that, Joe made coffee for her and brought it to her.

"Thanks so much, Joe," Katie said. "Oh, I forgot. You don't drink coffee. I'm sorry. I don't have anything else to drink except soda and water."

"No need to be sorry. I'm perfectly happy with water. We can pick up something later."

Joe went back to the kitchen and checked the fridge. It was very sparse. He found some eggs, butter, and milk that still seemed good. He checked the cabinets and found cinnamon. He was one ingredient short, so he kept looking. He was about to give up when he spotted it. Deep in the back of the cabinet was an unopened bottle of real maple syrup.

He mixed the ingredients and dipped a few pieces of bread into the mixture before putting them in the pan. When he finished cooking, he put the French toast on two plates and brought one of them, along with silverware and syrup, into the bedroom where Katie was. "I didn't want to interrupt you, but I thought you could use some breakfast," Joe said.

"Oh, that is very sweet of you, Joe, but I can take some time to eat breakfast with you." She brought her plate into the dining room and sat beside Joe while they enjoyed breakfast.

Joe said, "I know you can't bring me to your work every day, so I'm okay with staying here."

"I'll tell you what," Katie said. "You can ride with me to the station and wait outside. If I can get an assignment with someone cool, like Ashley, you could probably come along. If not, you will be on your own."

"I think that's worth the risk," Joe said.

After breakfast, Joe cleaned the kitchen, and Katie finished getting ready. Joe grabbed his camera, and they got in Katie's car. It was less than a two-mile drive to the television station. When they arrived, Katie went inside, and Joe waited by the car. There wasn't much to do in the area. The television station was a large, two-story building with several satellite dishes on the roof and a broadcasting tower behind it. Across the street was a large apartment complex, and next to that was a fire station.

The weather had warmed to just above freezing in the sun, and the streets were wet with melted snow. Even so, it was still cold outside, so Joe snapped a few pictures and then decided to wait in the car.

When Katie got to her desk, she checked her computer for messages. She wasn't there a full minute before she heard her boss calling for her from across the room. She stood up and saw Robert Martin waving her to his office. Katie walked to his office, and Martin handed her a printout. He said, "We have a double murder at Veterans Park. Grab Ashley and get over there as quickly as you can."

Katie found Ashley pouring a cup of coffee and said, "We got a hot one. We need to go."

Ashley put the cup down, followed Katie to the exit, and asked, "What is it?"

"A double murder. I'll tell you on the way."

When they got outside, Katie said, "Joe is here. I want to bring him along. Is that okay?"

"Wow! Things are really getting serious," Ashley said. "Sure. I don't mind. I just hope you don't do something to sabotage this one. I think he's a keeper."

"Would you stop? I don't sabotage relationships. Just get the van, and I'll go get Joe."

They split up, and Katie walked to her car. When she got close enough, she waved at Joe and motioned for him to follow her. Joe grabbed his camera, got out of the car, and followed Katie to the parking garage exit. They arrived just as Ashley exited the garage and pulled up alongside them with a news van. The van was modern-looking, with a retractable dish antenna on top. Katie opened the side door and said to Joe, "Sorry, but the van was meant for two people."

Joe looked inside and was very impressed. There was a large panel with hundreds of buttons and switches. Above the panel hung several monitors. There were also two chairs with wheels on them. Not exactly the safest way to travel, but at least they clipped to the side of the van while driving. "Very impressive," Joe said as he stepped inside.

Katie got in the front seat while Joe sat on one of the chairs. "Don't touch anything," she said, "and hang on."

They drove quickly, but another news team beat them to the scene. Ashley parked the van behind the other news van. Her camera was secured in a box behind the driver's seat, so she unpacked it, and the three of them started walking to the place of the murder. They had to walk almost a quarter mile down a pedestrian path before getting to where the bodies were found. On the way, they had to step out of the way so the coroner's van could get by.

Police tape was wrapped around several trees, and there were at least ten police officers inside the taped-off area. Katie showed her press badge to one of the officers on the scene and asked, "Who's in charge here?"

The officer pointed to his right, "That would be Lieutenant Garcia."

Katie saw that the other reporter was already talking to him. They approached just when their interview finished. Ashley raised her camera and said, "Okay, we're recording. "

Katie walked up to the lieutenant and said, "Hello, Lieutenant, I'm Katie Kowalczyk with Channel 23 News. Can you tell us what happened here?"

The lieutenant was a middle-aged man, perhaps forty-five, but Katie thought he was a good example of someone who could look good while still showing his true age. "It looks like a mugging gone wrong," Lieutenant Garcia said. "The victims were missing cash and credit cards. They probably resisted and got shot."

While Katie was interviewing the lieutenant, Joe was taking photographs of the scene, including the two bodies that were covered with sheets. He also took a photo of Katie, Ashley, and the lieutenant. He thought Katie might like to have a picture of her first serious interview.

"Can you tell us the names of the victims?" Katie asked.

"Not until after we notify the next of kin," Lieutenant Garcia said. "We will inform your news department as soon as that happens."

"Do you have any leads on who might have done this?" Katie asked.

"Not at this time, but we are still early in the investigation."

"Were there any witnesses?"

"We talked to some people who heard shots but were too far away to see anything. As I said, the investigation is just starting, and I expect we will learn more soon."

"How many shots were fired?" Katie asked.

"Our witnesses heard two shots."

"Thank you for your time, Lieutenant," Katie said. She turned to the camera and said, "This is Katie Kowalczyk reporting for Channel 23 News." Ashley took the camera off her shoulder and packed it into its bag.

"By the way," Lieutenant Garcia said. "I watch your news program and like your personal interest segments. Have you ventured into more serious subjects?"

"Yes. I've moved up into the investigative reporter position."

"Too bad," he said before walking away.

Joe was looking through the photos he had just taken and enlarged one of them. He showed it to Katie and said, "Look at this."

Katie looked and saw an enlarged section of the photo showing the man's left hand. "It's a picture of the man's hand. What am I supposed to see?"

"You're the investigator. Look closely. What do you see?"

Katie looked again and said, "I see the man's wedding ring and watch. It looks like a Rolex."

"So, what does that tell you?"

Katie thought for a moment, and then it hit her. "My God! This wasn't a mugging. Whoever did this took their money to make it look like a random crime, but they weren't thinking like a mugger or muggers."

"I think you have a story here, Katie Kowalczyk."

When they got back to the station, Katie invited Joe inside. She asked for his memory card. He removed it from his camera and gave it to her. She plugged it into her computer and found the photo of the hand. She cropped it as much as she could and then printed it. She gave Joe his memory card back, retrieved the print from the printer, and took it to Martin's office.

"Hello, Katie," Martin said. "How did your first real news story go?"

"They are calling it a mugging gone wrong. Look at this," she said while handing him the photo.

He looked at the photo and said, "What's this?"

"The victim was still wearing his wedding ring and Rolex. We didn't see the wife's hand, but I'm willing to bet her wedding ring is still on her finger, too."

"Muggers don't miss things like that," Martin said. "Good work. Stay on it. Find out what's going on."

"I will, sir. Thank you."

"By the way, where did you get the photo?"

Katie stumbled over her words. "Well, uh, I have a friend visiting from out of town. He doesn't have a car, and I felt bad leaving him home all day. He's a great photographer, though, and very smart. I thought he might be helpful."

"It looks like, in this case, he was helpful. Is he here now?"

"Yes, sir. He is."

"Bring him in here. I want to talk to him."

Katie hesitated but left the office and asked Joe to return with her to Martin's office. Katie walked into the office, followed by Joe, and said, "Joe, this is my boss, Robert Martin. Mr. Martin, this is Josip Novak."

They shook hands, and Martin said, "Pleased to meet you, Joe. Please, sit down."

Katie and Joe sat on chairs across from Martin's desk, and Martin said, "Joe, Katie said you are good at photography. The picture you took was very helpful, but noticing something was off with it was really impressive. Which one of you noticed that?"

Joe and Katie looked at each other, and Katie said, "Joe noticed it."

Joe said, "I showed it to Katie, and she figured it out."

Katie said, "Honestly, sir, I would have missed it if not for Joe. It's possible my reasoning skills are not up to the task."

"Nonsense," Martin said. "You used the word 'skills,' and that's what they are. Skills are something you acquire over time. What you learned today will help you with every story you do from now on. The same is true for what you learn tomorrow and the next day and so on."

He turned to Joe and said, "Mr. Novak, how long will you be in town?"

"I plan on going back home this weekend."

"Okay, I don't mind you hanging out with Katie while she works under two conditions. First, you can't do anything that will distract her from her duties. Second, you can't ride in company vehicles. We are not insured for passengers."

"I think those are reasonable conditions, Mr. Martin."

"Please, call me Bob," he said.

Katie looked at him in shock. Martin noticed the look and said, "You can call me Bob, too, Katie. Everybody is always so formal around me. I never asked for it, and, quite frankly, it makes me feel old."

"Thank you, Mr. Martin, I mean Bob. I better get back to work now."

"Good idea," Bob said.

"It was a pleasure to meet you, Bob," Joe said as they left his office.

Katie found a chair for Joe and set it next to hers at her desk. "I can't believe you are already on a first-name basis with my boss."

"It appears you are now, too."

"Because of you. What is it that makes you so damn likable, anyway?"

"I don't know, Katie. Maybe people are attracted to hermits."

"You joke, but you may be right. I'm attracted to you."

Katie's computer made a notification sound. She checked her messages and saw the police had just released the names of the two victims, James and Mary Williams, ages 74 and 72. They also released their home address. Joe was looking at the monitor and asked, "Are you familiar with that area?"

"Yes. It is in a wealthy part of town." She checked the map and looked at the streetside view. The home was a large, colonial-style home with beautiful landscaping. "It looks like this couple had money," Katie said.

Joe leaned over and said, "Do you think they were after something bigger, like passwords to bank accounts or something like that?"

"Maybe. Who knows? Do you think there was more than one murderer?"

"Not necessarily. I used 'they' in a general sense. I think if this was not a random act of violence, there is a chance a couple of people were involved."

"How so?" Katie asked.

"Well, if this were an individual bent on revenge for a perceived misdeed, he would probably just find out where he or she lived and shoot them. This murder wasn't like that. Someone probably watched them, learned their routines, and then set a trap for them. They knew there were two of them, so they would probably assume they needed one to do the deed and another for backup if anything went wrong. The backup could also be the lookout. On the other hand, if this person was experienced with a gun, two people could mean twice the chance of getting caught."

"So basically, you are saying you don't know."

"Yes. I don't know. Everything is a guess right now."

"Okay, so let's look at it from a different angle," Katie said. "What kind of person or persons would want these people dead, and for what reason?"

"Most everything that happens in today's society usually comes down to money. Someone either wants money or is trying to prevent a loss of money. Maybe the Williamses knew something that could cause the killer to lose a lot of money or send them to jail if it got out. They might have also stood in the way of him making a lot of money."

"You're assuming it's a man," Katie said. "Women can be just as ruthless."

"I won't disagree with you there," Joe said.

"What if the victims had something he or she wanted but wouldn't give it up?" Katie suggested.

"That's another good possibility. It might be easier to learn what they had than what they knew. How much money do they have? Do they have kids? How did they make their money?"

"Those are all good questions. Let's start with something easy, like real estate." She went to the county appraiser's office and searched for properties owned by James and Mary Williams. She found their home and two other properties in Milwaukee. She clicked on each one and discovered they were small apartment buildings.

While Katie searched, Joe watched the screen and said, "Is that it? It hardly seems worth killing for. Besides, how does one acquire property through murder?"

"Only an heir can do that, and only if they can get away with it," Katie said.

"Are those their only properties?"

"Those are the only properties they own in this county," Katie said. "I don't know about elsewhere. It would take someone more skilled than me to research it."

"Do you have someone here that does research?"

"As a matter of fact, we do," Katie said. "She wrote the names on a piece of paper and said, "Follow me."

They made their way to the far corner of the room, where a young man sat tapping away at his computer. He was wearing wire-rim glasses and had somewhat long sandy blonde hair that looked like it probably did when he rolled out of bed that morning. Katie tapped him on the shoulder and said, "Hi, Billy."

He turned around, surprised, and said, "Oh! Hi Miss Katie. What can I do for you?"

Billy was young. Joe doubted he had been out of high school very long. Either that or he was a genius and graduated when he was twelve.

Katie handed him the paper and said. "We need your help. We need as much information as you can find on these people. We need bank records, real estate holdings, previous employment, social clubs, whatever you can find."

Billy looked at the paper and asked, "Is this the couple that was murdered this morning?"

"Yes, they are," Katie said.

"Okay, I'll look into it, but I have something ahead of you, so I won't be able to get to it until later this afternoon."

"That's fine," Katie said. "Just do what you can."

They returned to Katie's desk, and she said, "I think this is a good time for a lunch break. If you like Mexican, I know a good place near here."

"Mexican sounds good to me," Joe said.

***

They put their coats on and got into Katie's car. Five minutes later, they pulled into the parking lot of the Mexican restaurant. It was a stand-alone building with an outside seating area that was closed for the winter. Katie and Joe walked inside, and an attractive young woman greeted them. She grabbed a couple of menus and led them to a small table by a window. A young man brought them chips and salsa and asked if they would like something to drink.

"I would like a Tepache, please," Joe said.

"Of course," the man said and turned to Katie.

"What's Tepache?" she asked.

"It is a fermented drink made with pineapples," Joe said.

"That's right," the young man said. "It is made from the peel and rind of the pineapple. The parts most people throw away."

"Okay, I'll have that, too," Katie said.

After the man left, Katie said, "I suppose you have experienced a lot of different foods in your lifetime."

"I suppose that is true, but honestly, I have only left North America twice in my lifetime, not counting when I was in the Army."

"Only twice in the last eighty years or so? Really? So, I guess that means before you were a hermit, you were a homebody."

"I guess I am many "H" words: humorous, honest, helpful, handsome, and humble. Don't forget humble."

Katie laughed and said, "You can be humorous sometimes. I won't argue with that."

"Seriously, though," Joe said. "I think I have always been a bit of a homebody. My wife and I were busy raising children at first. Later, we just enjoyed hanging out together or in the company of our grandkids. We did buy a motorhome in the seventies and went through a traveling phase, but it only lasted a couple of years and was mostly in The United States and Canada. We went to Mexico a couple of times, but not in the motorhome."

"Well, maybe it's time to plan a trip," Katie said. "Maybe to the area where your family comes from."

"I would like that," Joe said, "but only if you accompany me."

"I'd love that, Joe. That would probably be the trip of a lifetime."

Just then, the waiter came with their drinks and took their order for lunch. "Katie sipped her drink and said, "Mmm, this is pretty good."

"Drink that every day, and you'll live to be a hundred," Joe said and laughed.

Katie laughed, too, then got serious and said, "It must be hard on you. I mean, outliving the ones you love must be difficult. Is that why you live like a recluse?"

63

"Do you mean a hermit?" Joe asked. "Despite what everyone thinks, I don't see myself as a hermit. I like my privacy, but I can also be a people person. I help out at the lodge and am very good at talking to people. People like me for a reason."

"I'm sorry," Katie said. "I didn't mean to upset you."

"It's okay. I'm not upset. The truth is, you are not entirely wrong. It hurts very much to love someone and then lose them. Maybe unconsciously, I try to avoid that potential for pain by avoiding relationships."

"'Tis better to have loved and lost than never to have loved at all," Katie said."

"I suppose Tennyson was right," Joe said, "but it is still difficult."

Katie put her hand on Joe's and squeezed, but said nothing. They were interrupted by the waiter bringing them their food.

"Saved by the food," Joe said.

After lunch, they returned to the station, and Katie went straight to Billy's desk to check his progress. He said, "Sorry, Miss Katie, but I am just getting to it now. Give me two or three hours. I should have something for you then."

"That's fine," Katie said. "Can you put the information into an email and send it to me when you have it?"

"Certainly, Miss Katie. No problem."

When they got to Katie's desk, she said, "There's not much we can do until we have more information. Do you want to see if we can talk to that Croatian woman now?"

"Yes. I would like that," Joe said.

Katie got out the paper with the woman's information and dialed her number. When the call was answered, Katie said, "Hi, is this Katarina Babic?"

"Yes, it is," the woman said.

"Hi, my name is Katie Kowalczyk."

Before Katie could say anything else, the woman said, "Yes. I know who you are. Are you ready to come see me?"

"Yes," Katie said. "I am with the man who is looking for information on his family. I will be bringing him along if that is okay."

"I look forward to meeting you both. Do you have my address?"

"I do," Katie said. "We will be there soon."

Katarina Babic lived in a subdivision southwest of the city. It was a small, one-story brick home with a one-car garage. The house had a large front yard and a wooded area behind it. Katie pulled up the driveway and parked behind a twenty-year-old Lincoln Town Car. Katie knocked on the front door and waited. After about a minute, an elderly woman answered the door. Katie guessed that she was in her early to mid-eighties. Her hair was primarily white, but some dark strands still ran through it. She had it mostly covered by a headscarf.

"Hello. Hello," she said pleasantly. "I hope you didn't have trouble finding the place."

"No problem at all, thanks to GPS. I'm Katie, and this is Joe."

"Hello, Ms. Babic," Joe said.

"Mrs.," she said. "I was married for fifty-seven years. Sadly, my husband passed away two years ago."

"I'm so sorry to hear that," Joe said. "Losing someone you love is terribly difficult."

"Did you lose someone, young man?" she asked.

"I've lost many someones," Joe replied.

She put her hand on his arm, studied his face for a moment, and said, "I am very sorry."

She led them to the living room and said, "Please, have a seat." It was a relatively small living room with a sofa against the wall opposite the front window. Joe and Katie sat on the sofa next to each other, and the woman sat on a chair to their left.

"Would you folks like something to drink?" she asked.

"No, thank you," they both said in unison.

"We are eager to learn what you know about the Healers," Joe said.

"What do you know about your family?" Mrs. Babic asked.

"Not much," Joe said. "My great, great grandmother died when my great-grandfather was born. You saw the letter."

"Yes, I did. So, tell me, did the letter refer to your great-grandfather, or did it refer to you?"

Joe looked at Katie and back at the woman. "What do you mean? Why would you ask a question like that?"

"I wondered why you were so interested in Healers. I realized the reason when I saw you. You're too perfect."

"What do you mean by that?" Katie asked.

The old woman looked at Joe and asked, "Does she know?"

Joe sighed and nodded. "Yes. She knows."

"What did I miss here?" Katie asked.

"Look at him," Mrs. Babic said. "He has no pimples, no scars, no freckles, no crooked teeth. Imperfections that a normal person would have are missing from him. Only Healers are like that."

"But I'm not a Healer," Joe said.

"You can heal yourself, can you not?"

"Well, yes, but I can't heal others."

Mrs. Babic thought momentarily and said, "I was born during the Nazi occupation of Yugoslavia. My parents held our family together until after the communist takeover, when they were able to get us out of the country to American-occupied Berlin. From there, we made it to The United States. I was not even four years old at the time.

"My father's mother escaped with us. Her husband died during the occupation. My grandmother used to tell me stories about the old days. Many of those stories were about the Healer who happened to be my grandmother's grandfather."

She got up, retrieved a scrapbook, and sat on the sofa next to Joe, who was sitting on the middle cushion. She put the book on Joe's lap and turned to the page with her family tree. She pointed to the name "Josip Novak" and said, "This was your father." She then pointed to another name, "This was my grandmother. Her father and your father's father were brothers, and their father was a Healer."

"This is so much more than I was expecting," Joe said. "Thank you for sharing this."

"Of course. You are family."

"Is it okay if I copy this?" Joe asked.

"Please do. It is my pleasure to share it with you."

Joe turned to Katie and asked her to take a picture of the family tree, which she did.

"You are here to discover why you can't heal others. Is that right?" Mrs. Babic said.

"Yes. That's right."

"As you know, this gift you have cannot save your life from a bullet to the heart or the brain or any other extreme trauma. That is probably what killed the last Healer. Traditionally, the older Healer would pass down his knowledge to the younger Healer. According to legend, there were times when as many as four Healers were alive simultaneously. Unfortunately, the last Healer died before you were born. Additionally, the small village from which the Healers come no longer exists. It was mostly wiped out during the Great War. The survivors scattered throughout Europe and the United States. It seems you are now the last Healer."

"Do you know anything else?" Joe asked. "How can I use my gift to help others?"

"I'm afraid I can't help you with that. You will need to discover that on your own."

"So your grandmother did not share that information with you?" Joe asked.

"I don't think my grandmother knew any more than I told you. She only knew that the healing took place through touch."

"Do you know anyone else who might have an answer for me?" Joe asked.

Mrs. Babic thought for a moment and then said, "I'm sorry. I don't know anyone else who could help you."

"That's okay. You have told me more than I could have hoped for," Joe said. He handed the book back to Mrs. Babic and stood up. "It was a pleasure meeting you, Mrs. Babic, but Katie needs to return to work. I greatly appreciate what you told me, and I hope to visit you again soon."

"I would love to see you again, too," said Mrs. Babic.

They said their goodbyes, and when they were back in Katie's car, she said, "That is incredible. I'm sorry you didn't get all the answers you wanted, but we learned a lot today, and you met a relative. That must feel good."

"It does feel good," Joe said. "I always assumed I would never know the truth about where I came from, but now, I feel like I am one step away from knowing everything. I just don't know how to take that final step."

"I have faith that you will figure it out," Katie said.

They headed back to Katie's apartment. On the way, they picked up a carton of orange juice and an order of Chinese food. They sat at the table eating while Katie checked her emails. She found an email from Billy and opened it. "It looks like the Williamses had just over sixty thousand dollars in their bank account. There hasn't been any change to the amount lately, so I doubt a bank password was the reason for their murder. They also have almost two million dollars worth of stock. Again, no recent changes."

"Do they have children?" Joe asked.

"Yes. They have a son named 'David,' but no address is listed for him."

"What about properties?" Joe asked.

"Well, besides their home and the two small apartment buildings I mentioned, the only other property is a two-bedroom home in Lake County, Illinois."

"I wonder why they own that," Joe said. "I mean, if you want to invest in real estate, why not keep them close together so you can manage them better?"

"I don't know," Katie said. "I think tomorrow we need to talk to people who knew them."

"I agree," Joe said. "We can start with their neighbors."

Joe collected all the trash when they finished eating and threw it away. He then washed the dishes and held out his hand for Katie. "We need to get an early start tomorrow, so we should go to bed now."

"It's only seven o'clock, Joe."

"I said 'go to bed,' not 'go to sleep.'"

Katie smiled, took Joe's hand, and let him lead her into the bedroom.

# Chapter 12

The next morning, Joe made breakfast again while Katie got ready. They ate together like the previous morning, but this time, Joe had his orange juice to enjoy while Katie was drinking her coffee. When they were ready, they drove to the home of James and Mary Williams. They parked on the street in front of the house. It was an older neighborhood. Most of the homes were at least forty years old, but the residents kept the neighborhood looking good.

Katie grabbed a notepad before they got out of the car and headed to the home on the left. She rang the doorbell, and an older woman, perhaps sixty, answered. She had short, wavy hair that was colored an unnatural-looking orange. "Can I help you?" she asked.

Katie said, "Hi, my name is Katie, and this is Joe. We are with Channel 23 News. We would like to talk to you about your neighbors, James and Mary Williams, if you don't mind."

"Oh, I heard about what happened on the news. It was a terrible tragedy," she said. She then looked closer at Katie and said, "It was you I saw on the television talking to that policeman. Did they find out who did it?"

"No. Not yet," Katie said. "Can you think of anyone who would want to hurt them?"

"Absolutely not. They were the nicest people I know. James was always willing to help a neighbor in need. I don't mean financially. I mean, if someone needed help mending a fence or working on an engine, he was there. He helped bring my groceries into the house when I sprained my ankle. Little things like that but thoughtful."

"What about Mary?" Katie asked.

"Mary was the outgoing one," she said. "At Christmas time, she baked and gave everyone on the block a tin of cookies. She also volunteered at the animal shelter several days a week."

"Do you know what they did for a living?" Joe asked.

"Before they retired, Mary was a schoolteacher, and Jim was a real estate broker. He dealt with commercial properties, I believe. I suppose that's why they invested in apartment buildings."

"Speaking of that," Joe said, "do you think there may have been a disgruntled tenant?"

"It's possible," she said. "They have had bad tenants in the past, but Mary never mentioned any recent problems, at least not to me."

"They owned a home in Illinois," Katie said. "Do you know anything about that?"

"Oh, yes. That's a bit of a sad story. They only had one child, a boy. I believe his name is David. Anyway, he was always a problem for them. He worked as an auto mechanic when he lived with them. He would blow his money on booze and gambling, and I don't know what else. His parents seemed to be endlessly bailing him out of one kind of financial crisis or another. Finally, they bought a house far enough away so he wouldn't be a problem for them. They told him he could live there for free but would no longer help him with anything else."

"That's a shame," Joe said. "I can't imagine what it's like to be burdened by your own family."

"Then you are one of the lucky ones," she said. "It happens all the time."

"Do you think he might have been involved in their murder?" Katie asked.

"I doubt it," she said. "I saw him as irresponsible but not crazy enough to kill his parents. Besides, he never comes up here to visit them. Of course, you never know with people these days."

"Thank you so much for your time," Katie said. "Could we get your name and number in case we have any other questions?"

The woman gave Katie her information, and Katie gave her a business card and asked her to call if she could think of anything else that might be relevant. When they returned to the car, Joe asked, "So now what?"

"The woman seemed to know everything about the Williamses," Katie said. "I don't think we need to waste our time with other neighbors. We should probably talk to the son."

"Should we drive to Illinois, or do you think he will be here?" Joe asked.

"That's a good question. Maybe we should talk with the coroner first."

They drove to the coroner's office and spoke to the medical examiner. He was an older man, clean-shaven, with short, thin gray hair. He didn't talk to them in front of the body like they do on television shows. Instead, he ushered them into his office and asked them to have a seat. "What can I do for you?" he asked.

"We just have a couple of questions about James and Mary Williams," Katie said.

"Oh, yes. That was a real shame," he said.

"Did their son come to look at the bodies?" Joe asked.

"It is my understanding that the son will be in tomorrow. We had their IDs, and the fingerprints matched, so we didn't feel we needed anyone to confirm their identity. However, we expect that the son will want to confirm for himself."

"Can you tell us how they died?" Katie asked.

"Gunshot wound to the heart," he said.

"Both of them?" Joe asked.

"Yes, both of them," he replied.

"How many shots were fired?"

"There was one bullet in each body."

"In your experience," Joe asked, "how likely would it be for a mugger to fire two shots at two people and have both hit the heart?"

"I would say the shooter was either very lucky or very good."

"We saw that the man was still wearing his watch and wedding ring," Joe said. "Was the woman also wearing her wedding ring?"

"Oh, yes," he said. "She had a watch on her wrist as well."

Katie looked at Joe and then back at the medical examiner. "Thank you so much for your time," she said.

When they returned to the car, Joe asked, "Do you think the police are investigating this as more than a mugging?"

"If anyone on the force has half a brain, they are," she said.

"Maybe we should talk to Lieutenant Garcia again to see if the police have learned something we haven't."

"Let's wait," Katie said. "I want to talk to the son, which will take the rest of the day. Also, an extra day or two will give the police time to learn more."

"Okay," Joe said. "I'm up for a ride."

Before they left, Katie used her phone to send an email to her boss. She told him what they learned and that they were heading south to talk to the son.

Once they reached the highway, Katie mentioned she was hungry and wanted to stop at a fast-food restaurant for a quick bite. Joe wasn't crazy about fast food, but he was getting hungry, too, and knew they didn't have much time to waste.

They arrived at their destination about an hour and a half after leaving Milwaukee. The home was in a town called Antioch, not far from the border. It was in the old part of town, near the downtown area. They pulled into the driveway of an older, two-story home with a detached garage in the back. Joe recognized the style and guessed it was built in the fifties or early sixties. Although it was old, it was in decent condition. It was not at all what Joe expected. Based on the stories he heard, he figured the son was a deadbeat who wouldn't take care of his property.

They got out of the car, and Katie knocked on the door. There was no answer. She knocked again, and they waited. They heard a voice say, "He's not home." There was a woman next door taking groceries out of her car. She had two paper grocery bags in her hands and called out to them, "He's at work."

Katie and Joe stepped off the porch and walked next door. Joe offered to take one of the bags, and she let him. They followed her into the house, and Joe set the bag on the counter. "Thank you," she said. "My name's Beth. I assume you two are looking for David."

"That's right," Katie said. "My name is Katie, and this is Joe. We are with Channel 23 News in Milwaukee."

"Oh, my!" Beth said. "What did David do to get so much attention from Milwaukee?"

"We are actually doing a story on his parents' murder."

"What? Oh my God! I didn't know. Of course, we only talk occasionally. He's pretty busy. That's a real shame."

"What does he do for work?" Joe asked.

"He's a mechanic over at Marty's Garage."

"Marty's Garage? Where's that?" Joe asked.

"Well, If you turn right on Main Street and then left on 173, it will be a mile, maybe a mile and a half on the right."

"Thanks so much," Katie said. "One more question. What do you think of David?"

"He's a decent guy. He's friendly when you see him, but he doesn't go out seeking attention if you know what I mean."

"Oh yes, I know exactly what you mean," Katie said, giving Joe a nudge on his side. "Thanks again for your help."

When they returned to the car, Joe asked, "Are you insinuating I'm anti-social?"

"In case you didn't notice, you live alone in a cabin in the woods."

"I like my privacy. I told you that. That doesn't make me anti-social."

"If you say so."

"I say so."

"Well, I guess that settles that," Katie said. "Keep an eye out for Marty's garage. I don't want to miss it."

They pulled into the parking lot of Marty's Garage two minutes later. They went inside, but nobody was there. There was a mechanic in the nearest bay working on a jeep. He was average height, a little pudgy, with a full head of graying hair. He wiped his hands on a rag and came inside the office. "Good afternoon," he said. "Can I help you?"

"Are you David Williams?" Katie asked.

"Yes. What is this about?"

"I'm Katie, and this is Joe. We are with Channel 23 News in Milwaukee. I first want to say that we are very sorry about your parents."

"Thank you," he said, "but why are you here? You should be talking to the police. I don't know anything."

Joe spoke up and said, "I'm going to be brutally honest with you, David. We don't believe muggers murdered your parents, and before we waste too much of our time, we need to eliminate you as a suspect."

"Katie looked at Joe in shock, but David spoke up before she could say anything. "Me? Why would you think I killed my parents?"

"You were painted as a troubled son who caused many problems for his parents," Joe said.

David had a resigned look on his face and pointed to the waiting area. "Have a seat," he said.

Katie and Joe sat down, and David sat in a chair opposite them. "You are right. I caused a lot of problems when I was young. Hell, who am I kidding? I was a mess at forty. When my parents gave me a house to live in and told me they would no longer help me with anything else, it forced me to prioritize what was important in my life. Believe me, it wasn't easy, and I hated my parents for abandoning me. Slowly, I realized that they were showing me tough love, and it worked. I cleaned up my act. I quit drinking and gambling. I even quit smoking. I still enjoy a cigar occasionally, but that's it."

"So why did you never visit them?" Katie asked.

"Well, I regret that now. I did talk to my parents on the phone occasionally, and they came to see me a couple of times a year, but honestly, I needed the distance. I couldn't risk falling into my old habits."

"I have to ask," Joe said. "Where were you yesterday morning?"

"I was here early, around seven in the morning."

"Can you prove that?" Katie asked.

"Sure," David said. "We have cameras. I'll show you."

He went to his computer and brought up the camera feed. He then found the video file from the previous morning and brought up the clip of him unlocking the door and entering the building. The clock at the lower left said 6:57 a.m.

"Okay, now that we know you were not involved, we need to find out who was. Is there anything that you can tell us that might be helpful?" Katie asked.

"I don't think so. I mean, my parents were good people. I can't imagine anyone wanting to do them harm."

Katie took out her business card and said, "Please call me if you think of anything."

"Of course," David said. He took one of his business cards and wrote his cell number on it. He handed it to Katie and said, "If you find out who killed my parents, please let me know."

Katie nodded, and she and Joe went back to the car. "Well, that wasn't very helpful," Katie said.

"We eliminated the son. I would say that we accomplished something."

"You were pretty hard on him in there, Joe."

"I have learned there is a time and place to sugarcoat things. I didn't think that was either."

"Well, you got him to open up, so I guess there is a method to your madness."

They got back on the road, and Katie realized she was low on gas, so she pulled into a gas station just before the highway. Joe pumped the gas, and they both went inside to use the washroom. On the way out, Joe noticed they sold boiled peanuts and asked Katie, "Do you like boiled peanuts?"

"I don't know. I never tried them?"

"You never tried boiled peanuts? You must have lived a sheltered life. I'm going to get you a treat." He paid the cashier, who scooped the peanuts into a cup and then wrapped a plastic bag around them.

Once they were on the highway, Joe opened the bag and handed a peanut to Katie. "Here. Try one."

Katie put it in her mouth and bit down. It squirted juice on her shirt, and Katie said, "Oh, shit! Quick, I need a napkin."

Joe looked around and, not seeing a napkin, said, "Oops."

"Oops? What do you mean, Oops?"

"Uh, I forgot to get napkins," he said, laughing.

"Don't laugh. This is not funny. I can't go anywhere with juice on my shirt."

Joe closed the peanut bag and took off his jacket. He then removed his shirt and patted the front of Katie's blouse. He made sure he touched areas that were not even wet, just in case. Their eyes locked, and they started kissing passionately. Katie felt the vibration of her tires leaving the road and quickly corrected the vehicle. "We can't do that while I'm driving," Katie said.

"I guess we'll have to wait until we return to your place."

"No. You are taking me out on a nice date tonight. You haven't taken me anywhere since we met, and no, the restaurant at the resort doesn't count."

"I would love to take you out for dinner, Katie, but you have the car, so technically, you would be taking me out."

"Don't get technical with me, old man. I'll drive. You pay."

"Okay, deal."

When they returned to Katie's apartment, she removed her shirt and looked through her closet for something to wear. "I don't suppose you brought any dressy clothes with you?" she asked Joe.

"Sorry. I've grown so accustomed to dressing casually that the thought didn't occur to me."

"Okay. Casual it is." She found a white, low-cut sweater and put it on. Joe put his hands on her arms, looked her up and down, and said, "Wow! All the men at the restaurant will be envious of me tonight."

Katie put her hands on his face and said, "If you think that kind of talk will get you laid tonight, you might be right."

Katie leaned in and kissed Joe. He kissed her back, and it soon became uncontrollable. Joe reached down and started to pull her sweater up. She helped him until it was almost over her head, but then backed away, pulled her sweater down, and said, "Whoa, Cowboy. Save that for after dinner. I'm gonna let you in on a little secret." She leaned forward and whispered in his ear. "You don't need to get me drunk."

"There goes my game plan," Joe said, smiling.

Katie patted his cheek and said, "You don't need a game plan when the game is rigged."

"So, where would you like to go tonight?" Joe asked.

"You mean you're not going to surprise me on our first real date?"

"Very funny. Considering I don't know the city and you will be the one driving, surprising you will be hard for me to do."

"Okay, I guess I will be the one surprising you."

They got in Katie's car and drove to an Italian restaurant about 5 minutes away. The place was near downtown, and since it was still a bit early, they were able to get a table immediately. They were seated near the window where they could watch pedestrians walk by. The restaurant was about half full. Most of the patrons dressed casually, but the servers wore white, long-sleeve shirts with vests and bow ties.

A young man came to their table, set menus in front of them, and said, "Welcome. My name is Antonio. I will be your server this evening. Can I get you something to drink?"

"I'm sorry, Joe," Katie said jokingly, "but you can't get orange juice here."

"The waiter said, "Oh, but you can. It's under the kids' menu on the back, but anyone can order it."

Katie flipped the menu over to the back and looked at the kids' menu. "I don't believe it," she said.

"We'll have two glasses of orange juice," Joe said.

"He's joking," Katie said to the waiter. She looked at Joe and said, "We did not come to a nice Italian restaurant to drink orange juice."

Joe laughed and said, "I'll have a glass of Pinot Grigio."

"I'll have the same," Katie said.

Joe whispered to the waiter loud enough for Katie to hear, "Better make it a bottle. I'm hoping to get lucky tonight."

When the waiter left, Katie slapped Joe on the arm, laughed, shook her head, and said, "You are so bad."

Joe laughed, saying, "Maybe next time you will think twice before making fun of a man's orange juice."

Katie put her hand on Joe's hand and said, "I really enjoy being with you, Joe. These last few days have been wonderful. Of course, I'm not counting that first night when I thought I would be responsible for killing you."

Joe smiled and said, "I have had an equally wonderful time with you, Katie, and I'm also not counting that first night."

Just then, the waiter showed up with a bottle of wine. He turned over the wine glasses on the table and poured a little wine into each. He then set the bottle on the table and asked, "Have you folks had a chance to look over the menu?"

"Joe said, "I'm sorry. We were too busy flirting. Can you give us a couple of minutes?"

"Of course," he said before walking away.

Katie playfully slapped Joe's arm again and said, "I can't take you anywhere."

Joe picked up his wine glass and said, "To happy endings."

"To happy endings," Katie said, and they clicked their glasses together and took a sip of the wine. She put her glass down and asked, "Is this a happy ending?"

"What do you mean?"

"I mean, you are going back home this weekend. What does that mean for us?"

Joe took both of her hands in his, looked her in the eyes, and said, "Fate brought us this far. I like to believe fate will take us the rest of the way."

She looked at him momentarily and then said, "Are you always this optimistic?"

"Not always. You saw the pessimistic side of me, but I have learned that good things happen more often when you believe than when you don't believe. I want good things to happen between us, so I choose to believe it will."

"You are very wise, Joe."

"A hundred years will do that to a man," Joe said. "Maybe we should look at the menu now."

They both opened their menus thirty seconds before the waiter came back. "Have you folks decided?"

"Yes. I will have the Chicken Cacciatore," Katie said.

"I'd like the Eggplant Parmesan," said Joe.

"Excellent. I will put these orders in for you."

"Thank you," Joe said.

When the waiter left, Katie asked, "Have you given any thought to our case?"

"Our case. I like that," Joe said. "Working with you as part of a team feels good."

"I like it too, Joe. Too bad it's only temporary."

"You never know what fate will bring. We could be working together as a team in the future."

"I hope you're right, but what about this case?"

"Well," Joe said, "I think money or stocks were not the motive since none were taken. We ruled out the son. They didn't steal keys and break into their house. Real estate is the only thing left of value."

"How do you think their properties are connected?"

"I would guess if it is real estate, then only one of their properties would be important. It's unlikely either of their houses would get them killed, so I think we should look closer at the apartments."

"I don't know what I will do when you are gone," Katie said.

"Don't sell yourself short, Katie. You are quite intelligent. You only lack experience. That will come with time."

When they finished dinner, they headed back to Katie's apartment. They barely had their coats off when the passion flared up again. Joe pulled Katie's sweater up and over her head. This time, she did not try to stop him. He removed her bra while she unbuttoned his shirt. She led him to the bedroom, where she removed the rest of his clothes and slowly moved her hands down the length of his body, admiring the perfection. She briefly entertained the idea that he was the reincarnation of Adonis.

They made passionate love and then lay in each other's arms. Joe said, "When we were making love, for a brief moment, I felt a deeper connection with you than I have ever felt with anyone, even my wife."

"I felt it, too," Katie said. "It was amazing. For a few seconds, it felt like we were one person. What do you think it means?"

"I don't know," Joe said. "Maybe this is what love is supposed to feel like."

# Chapter 13

Thursday morning was a repeat of the previous morning. Joe made breakfast while Katie got ready, but something felt different. Katie could sense that Joe was distracted. When she sat down to eat, she said, "What's wrong, Joe?"

"Nothing. Why do you think something's wrong?"

"Well, you haven't said much this morning, and it seems your mind is elsewhere."

Joe sighed and said, "I don't know. I guess I feel like a bad person."

Katie held his hand and said, "You are not a bad person. Why would you think such a thing?"

"I loved my wife very much. We were soulmates. At least, I thought we were soulmates. I never thought I was capable of loving someone like I loved her. That is why my relationships with women have always been casual, if you can even call them relationships. Then you come along, and in less than a week, I am experiencing things I never experienced with my wife. How does that not make me a bad person? Maybe I never really loved her. Maybe I just thought I did."

Katie got up and stood behind Joe. She wrapped her arms around him and said, "I honestly believe that if you think you love someone, you do. I should probably tell you now, Josip Novak, that I think I love you."

Joe stood up and looked Katie in the eyes. "I think I love you, too, Katie Kowalczyk."

They kissed for a long moment, and then Katie said, "You are a good man, Joe. What we shared last night was unique. It was probably because of your increased awareness of the abilities locked inside you. Perhaps one day you will discover the key."

"You are quite wise for your age, young lady," Joe said.

"Young? Ha! I happen to be thirty. Did you forget already?"

"Oh, thirty. That's right. Maybe it's time to buy a condo in Florida."

"Joke all you want, but you have no idea what it's like to be past your prime."

"Tell me, Katie, when was your prime?"

Katie looked at Joe, smiled, and said, "It was last night when we were together. See? I'm past it."

"You are a funny, old, past-your-prime woman, Miss Kowalczyk. It has been a long time since I smiled as much as I have these last few days."

"I feel the same way. I guess we are good for each other."

"I guess we are," Joe said. "Now, I think we should get ready so we can get to work."

"Look at you. All eager to work, and you're not even getting paid."

"I get to spend time with you," Joe said. "That's payment enough. Plus, who doesn't like a good mystery?"

When Katie and Joe got to the station, they went straight to see Billy. Katie tapped him on the shoulder, and he almost jumped out of his chair. "Oh, Miss Katie," he said. "What can I do for you?"

"I'm following up on the information you sent me about the Williams couple. I need more information on the two apartment buildings that they own. I need to know if there is anything special or unusual about them."

"I'm not sure what you mean. Can you be more specific?"

"Not really," Katie said. "We think their murder was connected to one or both of those apartment buildings, but we don't know how it was connected."

"We?" Billy said, looking at Joe.

"I'm sorry, Billy. This is my new partner, Joe."

They exchanged greetings, and Katie said, "Now, do you think you can get something for us today?"

"If there is something to find, I'll find it for you."

"Good. Thank you, Billy."

They went to Katie's desk, and Joe asked, "Where should we go first?"

Katie dug through her papers and found the addresses of the two apartments. "Well, one apartment is on 23$^{rd}$ Street, and one is on 38$^{th}$ Street. The 23$^{rd}$ Street one is closer, so let's go there first."

They got in Katie's car and headed to the first apartment. They parked on the street next to an old brick building on a corner lot. It had three floors, but one floor was partly underground, like a basement. Its windows seemed to peek over the top of the snow. A man, perhaps in his early thirties, was sitting on the stairs, drinking a beer and smoking a cigarette. Katie looked at Joe and said, "If I ever do that at ten in the morning, just slap me."

They got out of the car and approached the man. "Hi. I'm Katie, and this is Joe. We are with Channel 23 News. Would you mind talking to us about Mr. and Mrs. Williams?"

"The landlords? What about 'em?"

"Did you hear about what happened to them?" Katie asked.

"No. What happened?"

"Someone murdered them the other day," Katie said.

"No shit?" the man said. "Well, I'm sorry to hear that, but karma will get you every time."

"Karma?" Joe asked.

"Yeah. You know. When you do bad things, the universe gets you in the end."

"What bad thing did they do?" Katie asked.

"They just wasn't good people. First of all, they imposed all these stupid rules just to make themselves feel powerful or something."

"Like what?" Joe asked.

"Like smoking. They told us we weren't allowed to smoke in our own apartments. What kind of shit is that? I'm paying rent. I should be able to do what I want in my own damn apartment."

"You're out here smoking," Joe said. "Why do you obey the rule if you think it's wrong?"

"I don't smoke out here for them. I smoke out here out of respect for my girlfriend. She seems to think it's bad for the baby."

"I see," Katie said. "Is there anything else they did that would be considered bad?"

"Yeah. They actually threatened to evict us after being one month late with the rent. One lousy month. Can you believe that shit?"

"Those tyrants," Joe said sarcastically.

Katie kicked him on the shin and gave him a dirty look.

Oblivious to the sarcasm, the man said, "That's right, man. You understand."

"One more question," Katie said. "Have you noticed anything unusual or out of the ordinary around here lately?"

"No. Nothing comes to mind at the moment."

"Thanks so much for talking with us," Katie said before she and Joe returned to the car.

Katie said, "I'm not sure what we are looking for here."

"I don't know either," Joe said. "I was hoping something would jump out at us, but nothing seems to be jumping so far. Let's drive around the block."

Katie started the car up and slowly drove down the street. There were several houses after the apartment, and then another similar-looking apartment building at the other end of the block. As they drove by, Joe noticed a classic black Corvette parked on the street in front of the building. "I used to have one of those," he said.

"A Corvette?" Katie asked.

"Yes. That's a 58. I had the same year, except mine was red. It was my midlife crisis car."

"You had a midlife crisis, Joe? I find that hard to believe."

"Really? Why is that?" he asked.

"Because people have a midlife crisis when they realize they are getting older, and half their life has slipped away. They want to do something that puts a little spark back in their life before they are too old to enjoy it. You never had to worry about any of that."

"I told you before that I am not immortal. I've always known that I could die at any time. I've been lucky so far, but my luck won't last forever."

"I'm sorry, Joe. I hadn't considered that."

"I don't worry about death as much as I used to. I mean, I don't want to die, but when it happens, I will know I had a good, long, and happy life."

"Let's talk about something besides death," Katie said as they made their way around to the other side of the block. "What do you think of this area?"

Joe said, "It's not a bad area, but it's nothing to write home about either. I can't see what's special about it."

"I don't know either," Katie said. "Let's look at the other apartment building."

The other apartment building was very similar to the first one. It was an older three-story brick building, like the first apartment building, but this one did not have basement apartments. It was also deeper than it was wide. When they arrived, they saw a young mother strapping a small child into a car seat.

They walked over to her, and Katie said, "Hi. We are from Channel 23 News, investigating what happened to your landlords. Do you have a minute to talk?"

"Sure. I was shocked when I heard the news. Did they catch the killer yet?"

"No, they haven't. Not yet, anyway," Katie said. "Can I ask what you thought of Mr. and Mrs. Williams?"

"I thought they were very nice people, especially Mrs. Williams. Before little Christine was born, Mrs. Williams hand-delivered a present for the baby. It wasn't a cheap present. It was a good-quality baby crib. You know those can be expensive."

"Do you know anybody who might have wanted to harm them?" Katie asked.

"No. Everyone here liked them, as far as I know. I thought it was just a random mugging. Was it not?"

"We are just investigating all possibilities," Katie said.

"Has anything changed with this property recently?" Joe asked. "Have you seen anything unusual?"

"No. Nothing has changed around here in a long time," she said.

"Are you happy here? Joe asked. "I mean, is this a good place to live?"

"We are happy here. Sure. Of course, my husband and I would prefer to own our own home, but for now, this place is fine. Everything works, and if something breaks, they usually have someone out to fix it in a reasonable time."

"Okay," Katie said. "Thank you for your time."

They returned to the car and drove around the block, looking for something but unsure of what they were looking for. They drove back to the television station and checked to see if Billy had found anything.

"This is a tough one, Miss Katie," Billy said. "I didn't find anything useful in public records, so I checked recent news stories and social media posts. The only thing I could find was a single social media post from a man who lives two houses down from the apartment on 23$^{rd}$ Street. In his post, he says he was offered twice what his house is worth by a developer, but only if everyone on the block sells."

"Is that all he wrote?" Joe asked.

"That's it," Billy said.

"When was that post written?" Katie asked.

Billy checked his computer screen and said, "It was posted twelve days ago."

"That's good work, Billy," Katie said. Can you write down the man's name and address?"

"Sure, Miss Katie," Billy said. He wrote the information she asked for and handed it to her.

As they headed to the car, Katie asked, "Are you hungry for lunch?"

"Sure," Joe said. "What do you have in mind?"

"A little place not far from here serves great Chicago-style hot dogs."

"Sounds great," Joe said. "It's been a hundred years since I had a hot dog?"

"Really? Are you serious?"

"Well, maybe not quite a hundred years, but definitely more than six months."

Katie shook her head and said, "I'm tempted to make you walk there, Mr. Smartass."

The hot dog place was in a commercial area with several small shops and restaurants. They went inside and stood in line. They ordered two Chicago dogs and a large order of fries and sat down to wait for their name to be called.

"I'm curious, Joe," Katie said. "What do you normally eat when you are at your cabin?"

"It varies quite a bit," Joe said. "It depends on what my body needs, what I have on hand, and whether or not I feel like cooking."

"So, you can tell what nutrients you need and eat food that contains those nutrients?"

"In a way. I don't know specifically what nutrients I need. I mean, I couldn't tell you if I need vitamin C or vitamin B or whatever. I just know from experience what food will help satisfy a bodily need."

"What about hot dogs?" Katie asked.

"Well, there's a reason I haven't eaten hot dogs in six months to a hundred years."

They both laughed, and Katie slapped him on the arm. "Seriously, though," she said. "Is it bad that I brought you here?"

"You ran me over with your car, and look at me now. I think I can handle a hot dog."

"I didn't exactly run you over," Katie said. "Technically, you went over my car, so I guess that means I ran you under."

"Either way," Joe said, "I prefer a hot dog."

Just then, someone called Katie's name, and Joe went up to the counter and brought the food back to the table.

Joe took a bite of his hot dog and said, "You're right. This is very good."

"Stick with me, and I'll have you looking my age in no time," Katie jokingly said.

"Unfortunately, it's not possible for me to look as good as you. I mean, look at you. You're gorgeous."

"Flattery will get you everywhere, Joe."

"I'm being serious, Katie. I am certain that there are more men envious of me being with you than the other way around."

"Well, thank you, Joe. I feel fortunate to be with you, and I think plenty of women are envious of me as well."

"Why don't we walk down the street together and see how many heads we can turn?" Joe said.

"You are too funny, Joe."

When they finished lunch, they returned to the apartment on 23$^{rd}$ Street. They parked in front of the apartment and walked two houses down to the address Billy gave them. Katie rang the doorbell, and they waited. After about thirty seconds, an attractive, middle-aged woman wearing an apron answered the door. She was thin with shoulder-length blond hair. The smell of cookies escaped through the door, and Katie said, "Oh, whatever you are baking smells delicious."

"I'm making chocolate chip cookies for our church bake sale."

"Oh, I'm sorry. My name is Katie, and this is Joe. We are with Channel 23 News. We are looking for Scott Cooper. Is he here?"

"Scott is my husband. He's at work. My name is Ann. Can I help you?"

"Maybe," Katie said. "We are investigating the murder of the couple who owned the apartment building on the corner."

"They were murdered? Oh, my. That's terrible. I mean, I didn't know them, but it's still terrible."

"Yes, it is," Katie said. "Your husband posted that you got an offer on your house, but it was contingent on everyone on the block selling. Is that correct?"

"Yes. As far as we know, everyone signed on to the deal except the couple you just mentioned."

"Really?" Joe said. "So, they were holding out?"

"From what I heard, they weren't exactly holding out. They just plain didn't want to sell. I guess they were concerned their residents would have nowhere to go. There is a housing shortage going on right now. Is that why they were murdered?"

"We don't know," Katie said. "That's why we are here. Do you know what the developer intends to do with the property?" Katie asked.

"They want to turn this entire block into a condominium project," Ann said.

"Who is the builder?" Joe asked.

"I think they are called Leed Real Estate Developers. Leed is spelled L E E D. That's why I remember the name."

Katie asked, "How do you feel about selling?"

"At first, I was against it. I like this neighborhood. We raised three children here, and we never had to worry about them. That's not entirely true. We did worry about them, but we didn't worry about crime or bullies or drugs or things like that."

"So, what changed your mind?" Joe asked.

"Money," Ann said. "The kids are grown. Our youngest just left for college in the fall. We really don't need such a big house anymore. When they raised their offer, we decided that we could move anywhere we wanted to, within reason, of course."

"How will you feel if the deal doesn't go through?" Joe asked.

"I think I would feel both disappointed and relieved. Moving would be a new adventure for us, but I would also miss this place."

"What about your husband? How would he feel?" Katie asked.

"He would be more disappointed than me, but he is easy-going and would be happy to stay here if he thought that is what I wanted."

"Thank you so much for your time," Katie said.

"What do you think?" Joe asked when they got back inside the car.

"I think someone holding up a big condominium project is a good motive for murder."

"I agree. Maybe you can look up who runs this Leed company."

Katie got out her phone and looked up the company. After a couple of minutes, she said, "It looks like the company is based in Chicago. The CEO is a guy named Robert Leed."

"Do you think we need to go to Chicago, Katie?"

"I think I need to give Mr. Martin a progress report first."

"You mean Bob?"

"Oh, yeah. Bob. That will take some getting used to."

"Before we go back to the station, you should call David Williams to see if he knows anything about this condominium project."

"That's a good idea," Katie said.

She looked for his phone number and when she found it she picked up her phone and dialed. "Hello," David said.

"Hi, David. This is Katie again from Channel 23 News. We just learned that a developer was looking to buy one of your parents' apartment buildings, the one on 23$^{rd}$ Street. Do you know anything about that?"

"No. That's the first I heard. I'm in Milwaukee now, arranging my parents' funeral. If anyone contacts me, I will let you know."

"Thank you," Katie said. "Do me a favor. If anyone contacts you about selling, tell them you will think about it. Don't commit to anything right away. Your parents didn't want to sell, and we need to find out if that had anything to do with their deaths."

"So, do you think this developer had something to do with their murders? Do you think he thought I would be easier to deal with?"

"That is possible, but it is also possible that we are barking up the wrong tree. If they do contact you, be cautious, but don't assume the worst."

"There isn't much I could do now anyway. I have a meeting with the lawyers tomorrow to go over the will. It's possible my parents left everything to charity. I won't know until tomorrow."

"Okay, David. Please call me when you know more."

They drove back to the station and went straight to Mr. Martin's office. Katie knocked, and he waved them inside. "Hi, Katie," he said. "Hello, uh, Joe, is it?"

"That's right. It's good to see you again, Bob."

"Mr. Martin," Katie said. "I'm sorry. I can't get used to Bob."

"Call me whatever you like, Katie. Did you learn anything new you want to tell me about?"

"Yes, sir. We learned that a developer from Chicago wants to build a condominium project on the block where one of the apartments belonging to the Williamses is located. More significantly, we learned they were the block's only holdout. Everyone else signed contracts to sell."

"So, you think holding up a multi-million dollar project is a motive for murder? I would agree, but we need more than that."

"That's why I would like to go to Chicago tomorrow and talk to this developer."

"Okay," Martin said, "but if you can't give me something actionable by Monday morning, I think we will have to put the story on the back burner and move on to something else."

"That's a tight deadline," Katie said.

"Yes, it is," Martin said. "Unfortunately, we need to get interesting content on the tube daily, or we will lose viewership. If we lose viewership, we lose money. Many little stories now are better than one big story that may or may not happen in the future."

"Okay. I understand," Katie said.

After the meeting, Katie and Joe walked back to Katie's desk, and she said, "I don't think we have enough time to solve this thing. Tomorrow's Friday, and I'm bringing you home this weekend."

Joe put his hand on Katie's shoulder and said, "Relax. I have faith that everything will work out for the best one way or another."

"I wish I could have your optimism, Joe."

"You can. Optimism is little more than a lack of worrying. If you don't solve this case by Monday morning, you will simply get another assignment. Is that so bad?"

"No, it's not bad, but I would feel like a failure."

"Why? I bet we know more than the police, and they have an experienced detective on the case."

"You always know how to make me feel better, Joe. I don't know what I will do when you are gone."

"I have faith that will work out, too. For now, let's enjoy the time that we have together."

"What did you have in mind?" Katie asked with a smile.

"You know what I have in mind. But first, since it is still early enough, I want to cook you a nice dinner. We'll need to pick up some ingredients on the way to your place."

They left the television station and stopped at a large Italian market on the way to Katie's apartment. Joe was not planning on cooking an Italian dish, but he was able to find all the ingredients he needed there.

Once they were back at Katie's apartment, Joe set all the ingredients on the kitchen counter, put down a cutting board, and started cutting beef into chunks. He then put the chunks in a frying pan as Katie watched. "Are you going to tell me now what you are making, or is it a big secret?"

"It's no secret. I'm making Hungarian Goulash."

"Oh, I heard of that, but I don't remember ever having it."

"Another first, " Joe said. "I learned this from my wife's mother. She came to America not long before my mother arrived here."

"Is there anything I can do to help?" Katie asked.

"If you want to help, you can cut up the onion."

"I'd be happy to."

Katie peeled the onion and cut it into slices. She then stacked the pieces and cut through them again. After several strokes with the blade, she screamed out in pain. "Ow! Shit!"

Joe whirled around and saw Katie holding her finger. He shut the stove off and checked on her. "Let me see that," he said as he held her hand.

Katie let go of her finger so Joe could see. It was bleeding, so he led her to the sink and put her finger under cold water. He gently put a little soap on the cut and rinsed it again. "You got yourself good," he said, "but it's not deep enough for stitches. Where are your bandages?"

"They're in the bathroom cabinet."

Joe went to the bathroom and found a box of various sizes of bandages. He picked the appropriate size and went back to the kitchen. He cleaned Katie's wound again, dried it, and covered it with the bandage. He then held her hand with both of his hands, closed his eyes, and concentrated.

Katie looked at him and said, "What are you doing?"

"I'm trying to speed up your healing."

Katie waited about fifteen seconds and said, "I don't think it is working."

Joe opened his eyes and said, "You're right. It's not working. I don't know what I'm doing wrong."

"You are not doing anything wrong, Joe. In fact, you have done everything right since the day I met you." Katie put her hands on Joe's face and kissed him. She pulled away and said, "Let's finish this great meal of yours."

"Okay," Joe said, "but I'll take it from here."

"That's fine with me. I'm happy to watch you work."

"Don't get used to it. I'm going to teach you how to cut onions, and you can help next time."

"Very funny," Katie said.

"No, I'm serious. You don't live a hundred years without learning the trick to cutting onions."

"I bet you've learned a lot of things in your lifetime."

"You are right about that. I want to show you a few of those things after dinner," Joe said with a smile.

"I look forward to that, you dirty old man."

Joe finished putting the ingredients together in the pot. When the stew was simmering just right, he said, "This needs to cook for at least ninety minutes."

"That should give us plenty of time," Katie said.

"Plenty of time for what?"

"Plenty of time for you to show me those things you've learned."

"I will need way more than ninety minutes," Joe said with a wink, "but I think I can hit the highlights."

"I'm sure you can. I can show you a few things I learned, too."

"This should be interesting," Joe said as he took Katie's hand and led her to the bedroom.

# Chapter 14

Joe awoke just before seven. The sun had not yet risen, but he could see light through the window. Some of the light was from the streetlights, but he could also see light on the horizon. He looked at Katie, who was still sleeping but had a smile on her face. He assumed she was having a pleasant dream. Her hair was a mess, but Joe knew that was the prettiest sight he would see that day.

He put some clothes on and made his way to the kitchen. He brewed a pot of coffee for Katie but decided to have a cup, too, even though he had never been a coffee drinker. He thought sharing a cup of coffee with Katie that morning would be nice. When the coffee finished brewing, he poured a cup for Katie and added a little cream, as he knew she liked it. He then poured a cup for himself and did the same. He tasted it but found it a bit too bitter and added more cream. That made it better.

Just as Joe sat down to drink his coffee, Katie appeared wearing an oversized t-shirt. "Your timing is perfect," Joe said. "I made you a cup of coffee."

"I see that. Thank you. I need it. I see you also made one for yourself. That's surprising."

"I thought it would be nice to have a shared experience," Joe said.

"We had a pretty awesome shared experience last night," Katie said. "Several times, if I recall."

Katie took a sip of her coffee and looked out the window. "Shit!" she said. "It's snowing."

"I see that," Joe said. "Why is that bad?"

"We're going to Chicago today. The last time I took a road trip in the snow, I ended up hitting someone?"

"Someone? Uh, I'm right here."

"I'm sorry, Joe. You know what I mean."

"Does the snow give you anxiety?"

"Anxiety? No. I just don't want to risk hurting another person."

"I think your concern for others is admirable, but you live in Wisconsin. Driving in snow is what we do here."

"I know. I'll be fine. It's not snowing that hard, anyway. I was just worried that it would turn into a full-blown blizzard."

"It's not safe for anyone to be driving in a blizzard," Joe said. "Doesn't your phone have a weather thingy on it?"

"Thingy? You mean an app?"

"Yes. That's it. An app."

Katie unlocked her phone and checked the weather app. After thirty seconds, she said, "It looks like Milwaukee will get about three inches of snow. Chicago is not expected to get any snow."

"So, it seems there's nothing to worry about, but if you prefer, I will drive."

"I thought you couldn't drive," Katie said.

"I told you I didn't have a car. I never said I couldn't drive."

"You mean you have a driver's license?"

"Of course I do. It's hard to live in rural America without one."

Joe took out his wallet and handed her his license. She looked at it and said, "This says you were born October 3$^{rd}$, 1996."

Joe smiled and said, "That means I'm dating an older woman."

"Very funny," Katie said, handing back his license. "Do you have insurance?"

He put his license back, pulled out his insurance card, and said, "Do you need anything else, officer?"

"Yes," she said. "I need you to put your hands behind your back. You're under arrest for too many wise-ass comments."

Joe did what she said, and Katie climbed on his lap and kissed him passionately. After thirty seconds, she pulled away and said, "Oh! Is that a weapon in your pants? Don't move. I need to see what you're carrying."

***

Two hours later, they were on the road to Chicago. The snow had diminished to light flurries, and Katie decided it would be best if she drove. "I'm glad you were able to get back on that horse," Joe said.

"Are you referring to earlier or now?" Katie asked.

"I'm talking about driving. You sure have developed a dirty mind."

Katie put her hand on Joe's knee and said, "I guess you are rubbing off on me."

"I could reply to that, but I won't."

Katie looked at Joe, shook her head, and said, "Now, who has a dirty mind?"

It took them over two hours to drive to Chicago. They arrived at their destination and parked in the building's parking garage. At over forty stories tall, it would have been prominent on the Milwaukee skyline, but its neighbors dwarfed the building in Chicago.

They checked the directory near the elevator and found Leed Real Estate Developers on the 34th floor. They got in the elevator and punched 34. It took several minutes to get there because the elevator kept stopping to let people on and off. When they got off, they saw the office they were looking for was almost straight ahead. Two large glass doors opened to a large, modern-looking office. Several pictures hung on the wall that were probably illustrations of some of their real estate projects. There was a reception desk in the middle of the room. Behind the desk on the wall were the words "Leed Real Estate Developers." Under that, in smaller letters, read, "The Leeder in Condominium Development."

Katie and Joe approached the young woman at the desk, and Katie said, "Hi. My name is Katie Kowalczyk, and this is Josip Novak. We are with Channel 23 News in Milwaukee. We would like to speak with Robert Leed."

"Do you have an appointment?" the woman asked.

"No, we don't," Katie said.

"I'm afraid Mr. Leed is very busy and is not available. If you want, I can check his schedule for Monday."

"We just need to ask him a couple of questions. It will only take five minutes," Katie said.

"I'm sorry," the woman said. "I can't disturb him."

"So, let me get this straight," Joe said. "When we do our report saying that the only people that refused to sign a contract with Leed Real Estate Developers were found murdered, you want us to put you down for no comment? Is that correct?"

The woman clearly did not know how to answer that and said, "Just a minute." She got up from her seat and went to the back.

"I like your style," Katie said.

The woman returned ninety seconds later and said, "Mr. Leed will see you now."

She led them to an office and opened the door. Katie and Joe walked inside and were greeted by an older man, perhaps in his mid-sixties, with short dark hair that grayed at the temples. He wore a black suit with a red tie. He stood up from behind his desk and said, "Welcome. I'm Robert Leed."

Katie and Joe shook his hand and introduced themselves. He then directed them to have a seat. There was a large picture window that Katie sat next to. She could see Lake Michigan and most of the city's southern half. "This view is fantastic," she said.

"I never get tired of it," Robert Leed said. "What is this I hear about a murder?"

"James and Mary Williams were murdered on Tuesday morning," Katie said. "They own an apartment building on a property that you need for your condominium project in Milwaukee. The only motivation that we could find for their murder is that they were the only people on the property that you need who refused to sign a contract to sell."

"Wait a minute," Leed said. "Are you accusing me of having something to do with their murder? I don't even know who these people are."

"We are not accusing you of anything," Joe said. "We are just following the clues, and one of those clues led us here. If you are innocent, we would love to be able to check you off our list."

"How many people are on your list?" he asked.

"So far, just you," Joe said.

Leed typed something on his computer and said, "I see them here. It is for a project on 23$^{rd}$ Street. It is true that they didn't sign with us. It is also true that this happens a lot. Often, we can persuade people with more money, but sometimes, we just have to move on to the next project. In this case, we have more than one potential site for this project. If we can't acquire what we need, we will move on to the next site. If that doesn't work, we will abandon everything and try again elsewhere. We have very little money invested here. If it doesn't work out, we won't lose much."

"Can we ask where you were on Tuesday morning?" Katie asked.

Leed pushed an intercom button and said, "Miss Jones, will you come here a minute, please?"

A few seconds later, the receptionist opened the door and said, "Yes, Mr. Leed."

"Can you please tell these people where I was Tuesday morning?"

"Mr. Leed has been here every morning this week," She said. "I come in at eight, and he is always here before me."

"Thank you, Miss Jones," he said.

She left the office, and Katie said, "Thank you for your time, Mr. Leed."

When they got on the elevator, Katie asked, "Do you think he's telling the truth?"

"His argument sounds reasonable," Joe said. "On the other hand, he may be a good liar. He also doesn't seem like the kind of guy who would do his own killing. If he is involved, he would have sent someone there to do his dirty work."

"Either way," Katie said, "we don't have a story. I failed my first assignment."

The elevator opened, and two men got on. When the elevator reached the parking garage, the two men got off. Katie started to leave, but Joe held her back, pointed to an advertisement in the elevator for a pizza place, and said, "Are you hungry? I think I know where we can get authentic Chicago-style pizza."

Katie smiled and said, "How often do I have to say it? You know the way to a woman's heart." She pressed the button for the sixth floor.

They ordered a small, deep-dish pizza and ate it near a window. The large building across the street blocked most of the view, but they were low enough to see dozens of people going about their daily business.

Katie took a bite of her pizza and said, "This is really good."

"Are you feeling a little better?" Joe asked.

"You mean about being a failure? Not really."

"You are not a failure," Joe said. "First of all, it's not Monday morning yet. Second, if we don't find the killer, that doesn't make you a failure. Thomas Edison once said about his light bulb, 'I have not failed. I found 10,000 ways that won't work.' Sometimes, you must fail in order to succeed. If we don't solve this case, you will at least have learned some lessons that you can apply to your next assignment."

"I suppose you are right, but this investigating business is harder than I thought."

"I'm sure your boss knows how difficult it is, so don't worry about your job. If you don't get this one, you'll get the next one."

"I hope so," Katie said. "I was going to ask you to stay this weekend and help wrap this up, but since we have nothing to go on, I think spending the weekend with you at your cabin would be good for me."

"I think that would be good for me, too," Joe said, "but I don't think you need to give up just yet. If you want to bring me home tomorrow, I would happily spend a nice, quiet weekend with you. If you want to stick with this case until the last minute, I will happily stay with you until then."

Katie leaned over and kissed Joe. "You are too good for me, Joe. Let's see what happens today, and we can decide what to do tomorrow morning."

"Okay. Whatever you decide is fine with me."

*** 

After lunch, they returned to Katie's car and drove back to Milwaukee. When they got on the highway, Joe said, "I guess this is a good time to check in with Lieutenant Garcia to see if the police found anything new."

"I was thinking the same thing," Katie said. "They may know something that will help us."

When they reached the police station, Katie told the receptionist who they were and that they wanted to speak with Lieutenant Garcia.

"He is not in at the moment. He's working on a case," she said.

"Do you have his business card?" Katie asked.

She pointed to the wall on Katie's left. "Everyone's business card is on the wall over there."

"Thank you," Katie said, and she and Joe walked over to the business cards and started looking through them. Katie found it first, took out her phone, and dialed Lieutenant Garcia's number.

"Hello. Lieutenant Garcia. Can I help you?"

"Hi, Lieutenant. This is Katie Kowalczyk from Channel 23 News. My partner and I are here at the station because we wanted to discuss the Williamses' case with you."

"I'm in the parking lot. Wait there. I will meet you in two minutes."

True to his word, he showed up in the lobby two minutes later. "Hello," he said. "It's good to see you again, Miss, uh."

"Kowalczyk," Katie said. This is my partner, Joe Novak.

"Nice to meet you, Joe," he said as they shook hands. "Why don't you two come to my desk?"

They followed him through a large room with many desks. About a third of them had police officers sitting in them. It reminded Katie of her office, but her office had dividers between the desks.

They sat in front of the Lieutenant's desk, and he said, "The Williams case has been put on the back burner. I'm working on another case now that takes priority."

"That's ridiculous," Katie said. "Two people were murdered, and you are going to sweep it under the rug?"

"It's not being swept under the rug. It has just become a lower priority."

"Do you agree with this priority?" Joe asked.

"No, I don't, but it wasn't my call."

"Whose call was it?"

"My captain decided it was a waste of resources. He thinks it was a random mugging."

"What do you think?" Katie asked.

"I think nothing was random about it, but it's not a democracy here. Besides, he may be right. I mean, it's unlikely that muggers would miss a Rolex watch and two wedding rings, but they might have been scared off by something."

"We found a possible motive for their murder," Joe said.

Lieutenant Garcia looked surprised and asked, "What did you find?"

"A company called Leed Real Estate Developers wants to buy up the entire block that one of the Williamses' apartments is on. We learned they were the only ones to refuse to sign the sales contract." Joe said. "The word is that Leed is offering far more than any of those properties are worth."

"So do you think someone at this Leed company killed them?"

"It's possible," Katie said. "We spoke with the CEO today, and he has an alibi. He also made a convincing argument. He says this kind of thing happens quite often, and they have alternate locations picked out. He could be a good liar. We don't know."

"The other possibility is someone on the block is unhappy with them," Joe said. "Maybe the possibility of getting double what your home is worth is a motive for murder."

"Very interesting," Garcia said. "I'll check into it. If it's true, maybe my captain will change his mind."

"What's your captain's name?" Joe asked.

"Matt MacKay. Why?"

"Just curious."

"Thank you for your time, Lieutenant Garcia," Katie said. She handed him her business card and said, "Please call me if you learn anything."

"Of course," he said. "Thank you for bringing me that information."

On the way out, Joe checked the rack with everyone's business cards. He found Matthew MacKay's card and put it in his wallet.

When they returned to the car, Katie said, "This has been quite a week. I think I just want to go home and veg out. Is that okay with you?"

"That's fine with me. I have come to enjoy hanging out at home."

"Maybe we can order Chinese food again and watch a movie," Katie said.

"That sounds great, but let's skip 'Highlander' this time."

Katie laughed and said, "I was thinking of 'Forever Young.'"

"Very funny," Joe said. "I was thinking of the movie 'Crash.'"

Katie put on a fake pouty face, but couldn't hold it and started laughing. She then picked up her phone and ordered Chinese food for pickup.

On the way to pick up the food, Katie's phone rang. She answered it and said, "Hello. This is Katie."

"Katie. This is David Williams."

Katie looked at Joe and hit the speaker button. "David. Hi. I have you on speaker. I'm here with my partner, Joe. What can I do for you?"

"Well, I saw the lawyer this morning, and my parents did leave me everything. I'm calling because I just got off the phone with a representative of the Leed Corporation. They offered me a significant sum of money for the apartment building you were talking about."

"What did you tell them?" Katie asked.

"I told them no."

"I thought we discussed that you would tell them you'd think about it. Telling them no might put you in the same danger as your parents."

"I realize that, but if my parents didn't want to sell, I want to honor their wishes. Plus, if I sell, I am giving the person or persons who murdered my parents exactly what they want. I can't do that."

"I admire your courage to do what is right," Katie said. "I would just watch your back for a while."

"I'm heading back home for a couple of days to catch up on some work, and then I will be back in town next week. Hopefully, if someone wants to do me harm, they will have trouble finding me."

"Don't assume that," Joe said. "Watch your back, keep your doors locked, and try to stay near other people as much as possible. People that you know, I mean."

"Don't worry about me. If they kill me, they won't be able to pass it off as a random mugging."

After Katie hung up, they picked up the Chinese food and headed to Katie's apartment. When they arrived, Katie set the food on the coffee table, and they browsed through the available movies together. They settled on "A Few Good Men" and sat together on the sofa while eating the food. When the movie was over, Katie was sleeping with her head on Joe's chest.

Joe slowly moved her to a sitting position without waking her. He cleaned up the mess, picked Katie up, and carried her to bed. She woke up briefly, asked if the movie was over, then fell asleep again. Joe slipped in next to her, put his arms around her, and fell asleep.

# Chapter 15

Katie woke up first the next morning. She could see light coming through her bedroom window, so she checked the clock. It was almost seven. She turned to face Joe, who opened his eyes, smiled, and said, "Good morning, Beautiful."

"Good morning," Katie said. "Did we really go all night without sex?"

"Let's not make that a habit," Joe said.

"So, what do you think?" Katie asked. "Should I bring you home?"

"I think we should stay here and see what we can learn today. We can revisit the question tomorrow."

"So, where do you want to start?"

"Let's go back to the scene of the crime."

"Okay," Katie said, "but I think you should take me out for breakfast first."

"So, you don't want me to cook for you this morning?"

"No. It's the weekend. You deserve to relax and let someone else do the work."

When Katie was ready, they headed to a nearby restaurant that Katie often ate at. It was the end unit in a small strip mall. When they arrived, the place was nearly full, but they were able to get a small table in the back. A middle-aged woman with her long brown hair tied back in a ponytail came to their table and asked if they wanted something to drink. Katie said she wanted a coffee, and Joe asked for an orange juice.

"Did you give up on coffee already?" Katie asked.

"I wanted to have a shared experience with you, which I did. Now that I accomplished that, I figured I could return to what I like."

"You don't like sharing experiences with me?" Katie asked.

"Of course I do. Wait. Are you pulling my leg?"

Katie laughed and said, "You're not the only one with a sense of humor."

"Oh, so you think I'm funny?"

"You do have the ability to make me smile from time to time."

The waitress came with their drinks and asked if they knew what they wanted. Katie ordered a Belgian waffle, and Joe ordered a veggie omelet. When she left, Katie asked, "Why did you want to stay? I mean, we could have had a nice weekend at your cabin instead of running around town on a quest for something we may never find."

"I didn't want you to return to work on Monday feeling like a failure. We may not learn anything new this weekend, but whatever happens, you will know you did your best and didn't give up."

"Katie put her hand on his and said, "Thank you, Joe. I would not have made it this far without your insights. I wish you could be my partner on all my cases."

Joe wasn't sure what to say to Katie. He wanted to hold out hope that a solution to their inevitable separation would present itself, but their time together was drawing to an end, and he wasn't sure a way could be found to stay together. Fortunately, the waitress showed up and said, "Your breakfast will be up in just a minute."

Finally, Joe said, "Katie, I don't know what the future will bring us. I don't know if I will always be able to work with you like this. What I do know is that I will always be there for you."

They were interrupted again by the waitress putting their food on the table. "Is there anything else I can get you folks?" she asked.

"No, thank you," Katie said.

There was an awkward silence, and then Katie said, "You will be two hours away. How exactly will you be here for me?"

"Things tend to work themselves out if you have faith," Joe said, unsure if he believed it himself.

When they finished breakfast, they headed to the scene of the crime. They parked in the same parking lot as before and walked the quarter mile to the crime scene. This time, the police tape was gone, and the place was almost deserted except for a couple of walkers who passed them on the way there.

The murder occurred near a group of trees just before the trail reached Lake Michigan. Joe walked to the opening near the lake and looked around. He then walked twenty yards in the other direction and looked around. "My guess is the murderer hid in these trees and waited for the couple to show up. The trail has a curve, so it is in a spot where nobody can see unless they are very close."

"It's too bad there aren't any cameras out here," Katie said.

"Cameras? You may be on to something, Katie."

"I am? What am I on to?"

"C'mon," Joe said and took Katie's hand. He led her back to the parking lot and looked around. A building stood next to the parking lot. It sold hot coffee, sodas, and snacks. Joe pulled Katie toward the building.

"Slow down," Katie said. "I didn't wear my running shoes."

Joe looked at Katie's feet and noticed for the first time she was wearing high-heeled boots. "We need to get you some comfortable shoes," he said.

Katie looked at her feet and said, "I paid a lot of money for these. What's wrong with them?"

When they approached the building, Joe saw two cameras, one on either side of the order window. They were set up to record the line of people from opposite directions. One of the cameras pointed directly at the parking lot. "Look," Joe said, pointing at the cameras.

Katie looked at the cameras and then looked back at the parking lot. "You're a genius, Joe," Katie said.

"You gave me the idea."

They approached the window, and a young man said, "What can I get for you?"

"We are with Channel 23 News," Katie said. "Are you aware of the murder that occurred here the other day?"

"Oh, yes. That's all anybody has been talking about lately."

"We'd like to take a look at your camera footage of the parking lot from that morning," Joe said. "There may be a clue as to who did it on those recordings."

"I don't know," the young man said. "I don't think I'm allowed to show those to people."

"Do you really think your boss would not want to help catch a murderer?" Katie asked.

"I just don't want to lose my job."

"Joe pulled a hundred-dollar bill out of his wallet and said, "Would this offset the risk?"

Katie looked at Joe with surprise, but the young man took the money and went around to open the door. He led them to a back office and accessed the video files on the office computer. "What day and time do you want to look at?" he asked.

Joe wasn't sure, so he looked at Katie. She thought for a moment and said, "The murder took place around six-thirty on Tuesday. Let's start around five forty-five."

"The clips are in ten-minute increments," he said. "How about five fifty?"

"That's fine," Joe said.

The young man searched for the correct clip and brought it up. It was black and white because it was using night vision. It showed the date and time in the bottom-right corner. Joe asked if he could speed it up. The man clicked a button a few times, and they watched it at ten times the normal speed, but saw nothing useful. The man then moved on to the next clip and watched it at the same ten times speed. About halfway through the clip, a car zipped by.

"Wait! Stop. Go back," Joe said.

He brought it back to just before the car went by and played it at normal speed. They watched a dark-colored, classic Corvette drive by and park at the far end of the parking lot. "Oh, my God!" Joe said. "We saw that car at that apartment building."

"Are you sure it's the same one?" Katie asked.

"Can you freeze on the car?" Joe asked.

The young man rewound the video and stopped as the Corvette drove by. Joe studied it for several seconds. "It looks like a fifty-eight. Just like the other one. How many of those do you think are driving around Milwaukee? Bring it forward a little. Let's see what the license plate says."

He played it forward and stopped when the license plate came into view. "Damn!" Joe said. "It's too pixilated to read it."

They watched the rest of the clip. After the driver parked the car, they observed a figure get out and walk down the trail. It was too far away to see any detail. They couldn't tell if it was a man or a woman. They didn't see anyone else get out of the car, so, assuming this was the killer, they now knew they were looking for a single suspect."

The following clip showed a sedan driving by and parking near the Corvette. Two people got out that Joe and Katie assumed were the Williamses. They walked onto the trail and disappeared. A couple of clips later, they watched the Corvette leave the parking lot but could not make out the driver.

Katie handed the young man her business card and said, "I need you to email those clips to me."

Joe slipped the man another twenty and said, "Thank you."

As they walked back to the car, Katie said, "I don't think you needed to pay that man."

"Maybe not, but it worked and was worth the money. Besides, he probably has more of a use for the money than I do."

When they got back inside the car, Joe said, "We need to go back to that apartment where we saw that car."

"I was thinking the same thing," Katie said.

When they arrived at the apartment building, the Corvette wasn't in the parking lot. Nobody was outside, so Joe and Katie went inside and knocked on the nearest door. They waited for a while and knocked again. They gave up and started walking towards the next door when they heard the first door open.

They turned and saw an old man appear in the doorway. He looked close to ninety and had a cane in his left hand. "Can I help you?" the man asked.

They stepped back towards the old man, and Katie said, "Hi. My name is Katie, and this is Joe. We are with Channel 23 News. We are looking for the owner of the old, black Corvette that was parked here the other day."

"Oh, that's a beautiful car, isn't it?" the man said. "I dreamed of having one like that when I was young, but I couldn't afford it on a painter's salary."

"Do you know who it belongs to?" Joe asked.

"Sure. That's the landlord's car."

"What is his name?" Joe asked.

"I'm sorry. I don't know that. I write my rent check out to the management company. The owner usually comes around when there is a major problem or if he has to meet with contractors or something like that. There's been a lot of those visits lately."

"Really? What kind of problems go on here?" Katie asked.

"You name it," the man said. "This place is old and due for a renovation. I guess the biggest problem is with the plumbing. It seems they are cleaning up after a plumbing leak every month or two. They also have a lot of electrical issues, and the roof needs to be replaced."

"How do you feel about living here?" Katie asked.

"I do okay here. If I were younger, I would move, but now it's easier to stay put. Besides, I have nobody around to help me move, and I'm certainly not going to go to one of those homes where old people go to die."

"I don't blame you," Joe said. "Keep your independence as long as possible."

Katie gave Joe a dirty look, then turned to the old man and said, "Thank you so much for your time."

As they walked back to the car, Katie asked, "What was that crack about independence? Do you think having a woman in your life will somehow tie you down?"

Joe looked surprised at the question and said, "No, no, no. That's not it at all. For most of my life, I have been concerned about people discovering what I am capable of. I fear that if that happens, I will be taken away and kept in isolation while men in white coats poke and prod me, trying to learn what makes me work. I don't see nursing homes as being much different, except nobody is trying to learn anything there."

Katie put her arm in Joe's and said, "I'm sorry. I shouldn't have jumped to conclusions."

"You should know I don't see being with you restrictive at all," Joe said. "In fact, it's quite the opposite. I have done more since meeting you a week ago than I have done for the last year or more. I feel like I am at the beginning of a great adventure."

They got in the car, and Katie said, "Yes, an adventure that will end when you return home."

She started the car and put it in drive. Joe wanted to say something, but he didn't know what to say, so they just drove in silence for a while. Finally, he said, "What should we do now?"

"You mean about the case?"

"Yes. I assume you want to research who owns that building."

"Of course," Katie said. "We can do that from my apartment."

They returned to Katie's apartment, and she opened her laptop and checked her email. She saw the email she asked for with the video files. They were not attachments but rather links, so she had to download each one onto her computer.

She then went to the county appraiser's website. She typed in the address of the apartment building and looked for the owner's name. "It's owned by a company called "MacKay Investments, LLC."

"That name sounds familiar," Joe said. "Can you find out who owns that company?" Joe asked.

"I think so," Katie said. "I'm just not sure where to go to look up business names."

She searched for where to look up business names in Wisconsin. After scrolling past a few websites subtly marked "Ad," she found the correct one and clicked the link. She then typed in the business name and read the results. Joe looked at the screen and said, "Matthew and Laura MacKay. I've heard that name before."

It suddenly occurred to Joe where he had seen that name before. He opened his wallet and took out the business card that he picked up from the police station. He showed it to Katie, who said, "Captain Matthew MacKay. Oh, my God."

"Oh, my God is right," Joe said. "We have to tread carefully here. We can't exactly march into the police station and accuse the captain of a double murder."

"We need more," Katie said. "What if we're wrong? What if there is an identical Corvette in Milwaukee?"

"You have a valid point. I think it's time to get Lieutenant Garcia involved."

"Do you think we can trust him?" Katie asked.

"I don't know," Joe said. "He did seem a little annoyed that he was ordered to put the brakes on the case. I think there is a good chance he wants to solve this as much as we do."

Katie took out her phone and dialed Lieutenant Garcia's phone number. When it started ringing, she hit the speaker button. It was answered on the third ring. "Hello. Lieutenant Garcia here."

"Lieutenant Garcia. Hi. This is Katie from Chanel 23 News. I'm here with my partner, Joe."

"Hello, Katie and Joe. What can I do for you?"

"Well," Katie said. "We need to see you. It's important."

"I'm home with my family today. Can it wait?"

Joe said, "Family time is important, and we hate to interrupt it, but we need ten minutes of your time. Fifteen tops. We will come to you if that is okay."

"Give me a moment, please," Lieutenant Garcia said before putting his phone on mute. After about thirty seconds, he said, "I'll meet you at your place. Give me your address."

Katie told him her address, and he said, "I'll meet you there in thirty minutes."

Joe put his arms around Katie and said, "We have thirty minutes. What shall we do?"

"Are you a hundred or seventeen? I think you have just enough time for a cold shower."

Joe laughed and said, "You mean you don't fantasize about being caught by a police officer?"

Katie put her hand on Joe's face and said, "I'm going to assume you are joking right now."

A half-hour later, there was a knock at the door. Katie answered and invited Lieutenant Garcia inside.

"Thank you for coming, Lieutenant Garcia," she said.

"I'm off duty," he said. "Today, I'm just Gabe."

"Okay, Gabe," she said. "We appreciate you taking the time to come here."

"So, what did you find that is so important?"

"It's probably better that we show you," Katie said. "Please follow me."

She led him to her dining room table, where her laptop was open. She clicked on a video file, and when it opened and started playing, she said, "This is a video from Veterans Park the morning of the murder. The video begins at six in the morning. Approximately thirty minutes before the murder occurred."

Gabe and Joe were standing behind Katie, watching the video. "What are we looking at here?" Gabe asked.

"Wait for it," Katie said.

After another minute, the Corvette appeared, and Katie hit pause. Gabe looked closely at the screen and, after several long seconds, finally said, "Holy shit!"

Joe said, "So, I guess you recognize the car."

"My captain owns a car like that, but it couldn't have been him. There must be another car like that in town."

"There's something else we haven't told you yet," Katie said. "Captain MacKay owns an apartment building on the same block as the Williamses' apartment building. We checked it out, and the place needs expensive renovations. He was just offered a hefty sum of money for a property that is probably a money pit, but the Williamses were keeping him from collecting. I think that's a good motive for murder. Let's also not forget he pulled you off the case for no good reason."

"Are you sure about your information?" Gabe asked.

"We found him and his wife listed as owners of the building," Joe said. "We also saw his Corvette parked in front of the building. That's how we put it together."

"It couldn't have been him," Gabe said again.

"I understand and respect your loyalty to your boss, but you need to look at the facts," Katie said.

"I am looking at the facts," Gabe said. "Here's a fact for you." He took out his phone, scrolled through recent calls, and found what he was looking for. "Here is the call I got Tuesday morning telling me there were two bodies found in the park. It came in at 6:45 a.m. The number it came from is the police station's number." He showed them the phone.

"How does that prove anything?" Joe asked.

"It was Captain MacKay on the other end of the line. He sometimes gets to work early to catch up on paperwork. He was there early that day and did not drive his Corvette to work. In fact, he rarely drives that car to work. He has a plain-looking white sedan. I couldn't tell you what make car he drives, but I know the Corvette was not there that morning."

"Well, that throws a monkey wrench into our theory," Katie said. "What do you think we should do now?"

"You shouldn't do anything. I need to figure this out," Gabe said. "We have the weekend. I will see if there is a similar Corvette registered in the city. There are a lot of cars in Milwaukee. There must be at least one more. I'll let you know if I find anything. You two should just enjoy your weekend and stay out of trouble."

"That's asking a lot," Joe said.

"I figured as much," Gabe said. "I'll be in touch. Right now, I need to spend some quality time with my wife. You two should do the same."

When Gabe Garcia left, Joe said, "He's right. We should put this case on hold and enjoy our time together."

# Chapter 16

"So, what do you want to do now?" Katie asked.

Joe put his arms around her and said, "Well, part of me wants to spend the rest of the day making love to you."

Katie smiled and said, "I bet I know which part. What does the rest of you want to do?"

"It's a big city," Joe said. "You must know some fun things to do around here. Maybe you can be my tour guide."

"I know a place you might like, Joe. Bring your camera."

Joe grabbed his camera bag, and they got in Katie's car. After a short drive, they were on the highway heading away from the city. "I hate to tell you, but the city is behind us," Joe said. "Where are you taking me?"

"You'll see," Katie said. "I think you will like it."

About twenty minutes later, they pulled into the parking lot, and Joe said, "The zoo? You brought me to the zoo?"

"Are you disappointed?"

"Absolutely not. This is great. I haven't been to the zoo in ages."

"So, I guess I'm getting to know you," Katie said.

"It would seem that you are," Joe said. He leaned over and kissed Katie. He then grabbed his camera bag from the back seat, took out his camera, an extra battery, and an extra memory card, before they headed inside.

The weather had warmed to the lower forties, and all the snow in and near the zoo had melted. They first saw the penguins, who seemed to be enjoying the weather. One was swimming back and forth as fast as it could swim. It jumped out of the water on each pass like it was playing. Joe got a kick out of it, set his camera for video, and filmed the playful behavior.

"Are you having fun?" Katie asked.

"Of course," Joe said. "This was a good choice. I don't know what it is about zoos, but it makes me feel like a kid again. I guess it is because my parents often took me to the zoo when I was young."

"What did you like best when you were a child?" Katie asked.

"I liked everything, but if I had to choose one, I would say the bears."

"Well, let's go see the bears," Katie said.

"Lead the way, my dear."

They held hands and looked for a sign pointing to the bear enclosure. They soon found it and walked in that direction.

They came upon the polar bear enclosure first. A large male polar bear was pacing back and forth. Joe snapped several photos and then said, "Amazing creatures. Did you know polar bears are the largest carnivores on land? They are even bigger than grizzly bears. Back in the 60s, I went to Canada to photograph them. Some of those photos ended up in National Geographic. I think I still have the issue."

"I'd love to see your photographs, Joe. When we return to your place, I'd like to spend time learning about your life. I bet you have some interesting stories. Maybe you will even show me your scrapbook."

"I think I am at a point now where I feel comfortable sharing everything with you. I'm sure I could tell you a few stories that won't bore you too much."

I'm sure you could, Joe. Right now, my stomach is telling me a story about how hungry I am."

They found a restaurant with better food than expected for a zoo. Joe got a salad with apples and Wisconsin cheese, among other things. Katie got an Italian sandwich. They sat inside at one of a dozen or so picnic tables.

"Thank you for bringing me here, Katie. This is a great place to come and unwind."

"I'm glad you are happy, Joe."

"I'm happy just being with you," Joe said. "I would have been just as happy staying home with you, Katie, but now we have created a new memory together. Thirty years from now, we can bring our grandkids here and tell them about our first trip to the zoo together. We certainly couldn't tell them about our day together at your apartment if we had stayed there."

"Grandkids?" Katie said. "Do you expect that we will have grandkids together?"

"Well, I said that in passing. I didn't really think about it, but who knows what the future will bring."

"But you've already raised your kids. Do you want to go through that again?"

"You say that like children are a burden. Do you not want kids, Katie?"

"I do, I think. I don't know. I mean, I just started this new job. How would I possibly juggle work and kids?"

"You should do what brings you joy, Katie. For me, my children have given me more joy than anything I did for work, but you are not me. That is something you need to think about."

"Okay, but not today. Right now, we should think about seeing the chimpanzees."

They spent another couple of hours visiting all the exhibits. As they left the zoo, Joe asked, "What do you want to do now?"

"Would you mind if we just pick up a pizza and go home? I know we had pizza the other night, but that was a good night, wasn't it?"

"Are you kidding? "I would give my right arm to repeat that night."

"Knowing you, it would probably grow back," Katie said.

They called in the pizza order and picked it up on the way to Katie's apartment. Joe had it on his lap while Katie was waiting for several cars to go by so she could pull out of the parking lot. Joe noticed it first. "The black Corvette! There it is!" he shouted as it went by. "Follow it."

Katie had her blinker on to turn left, but quickly switched it to turn right and pulled out onto the street. There was a blue sedan between them and the Corvette. After about a mile, the Corvette turned left, and Katie followed. When the car reached 23$^{rd}$ Street, it turned right. Katie kept her distance. When the car reached the Williamses' apartment, it slowed to a crawl and then sped up again. The person driving parked in front of the apartment owned by Captain MacKay.

Katie parked on the street near the center of the block. The last bit of twilight hung in the distant sky. Most of the light came from a nearby streetlamp. They watched as someone got out of the car and walked into the apartment building. It looked like a woman, but the distance and poor lighting made it difficult to tell.

"At least we have something to eat," Joe said as he opened the box.

"Perfect," Katie said. "Give me a piece. Oh, and there are napkins in the glove box. I put them in there after the boiled peanut incident."

Joe opened the glove box, took out a couple of napkins, set a slice of pizza on top of them, and handed it to Katie. He then did the same for himself and closed the box.

Katie took a bite of pizza and, after she swallowed it, said, "This is pretty cool. I've never been on a stakeout before."

"This is my first, too," Joe said. "I guess this is another first for us."

"We are racking up firsts this week," Katie said before taking another bite of pizza.

They both finished their first slice of pizza, and Joe had the box open, preparing to get another piece when Katie said, "Something's happening."

Joe closed the pizza box and put it in the back seat. They watched the person come out of the apartment building and walk down the sidewalk towards them. It soon became clear it was a woman when she walked under the street lamp. She was of average build and looked to be in her early to mid-fifties. Her blonde hair was tied behind her head. When she got close, Joe leaned over and kissed Katie. Katie kept one eye open and saw the woman briefly look into the car as she passed.

They stopped kissing when the woman had passed and looked back at her. She must have assumed they were teenagers making out because she kept walking without looking back. They continued watching the woman and saw her enter the apartment building belonging to the Williamses.

"What do you think she is doing?" Katie asked.

"I have no idea," Joe said.

"Do you think she knows someone who lives there?"

"It would be odd if she did, but who knows?"

"Maybe she's casing the place," Katie said. "Maybe she wants to know the layout so she can know where to hide and shoot David when he shows up."

"I think you are on to something, Katie, but not to shoot David. She would have no way of knowing when he would show up."

"What then?" Katie asked.

"I don't know. Maybe some kind of booby trap. I just can't imagine how that would work, though."

A few minutes later, the woman walked out of the apartment building and headed back toward them again. When she got close, Joe kissed Katie again until she passed. They watched her until she got into her car and drove away.

"Well, that was weird," Katie said.

"It sure was."

"I enjoyed my first stakeout with you," Katie said, "especially the kissing part."

"I liked that part, too," Joe said. "I bet most cops don't have stakeouts that good."

"Let's have another piece of pizza and then make out some more," Katie said.

"Another wonderful idea," Joe said as he reached for the pizza box.

By the time they returned to Katie's apartment, they could no longer contain their passion. They slowly left a trail of clothing behind them as they made their way toward the bedroom.

# Chapter 17

The sound of a phone ringing woke Katie up. She looked at the clock and saw it was after eight. The sound was coming from outside the bedroom. She wanted to get up, but Joe had his arm around her and held her back. "It's Sunday," he said. "It can't be that important. Just stay here for a while."

Katie turned around to face Joe and kissed him. She said, "It's after eight o'clock. Do you want to stay in bed all day?"

"Yes."

"I guess we could, Joe, but then you would have to give up things like eating breakfast and going to the bathroom."

"That's fine," Joe said. "I'd much rather lie here naked with you."

"Nude," Katie corrected.

"You got me on that one. I must be tired. You also got me thinking about going to the bathroom, and now I have to pee."

When Joe got out of bed, Katie whistled and said, "Nice ass."

Joe looked back and said, "I can't wait to hear what you have to say on the return trip."

Joe made breakfast that morning again. As they were eating, Katie asked, "What do you think we should do about what we saw yesterday?"

"What would you do if you were working alone?" Joe asked.

"I guess I would start by learning as much as possible about MacKay's wife."

"Your friend Billy is not available today, so how good are you at research?"

"About average. I can find stuff that's easy to find."

"Then I think we should start with the easy stuff," Joe said. After that, we can call Garcia and see what he knows."

When breakfast was over, and the table cleared, Katie got her laptop, and Joe sat beside her as she worked. She first went to Facebook and looked up Matthew MacKay. There were dozens of people with that name, so she carefully looked through them until she found the one she was looking for. His profile page showed a photo of him standing next to his wife. He looked relatively handsome with short, graying hair and a well-trimmed gray beard. His wife was also attractive, with her long blond hair hanging over her shoulders. Only the wrinkles next to her eyes gave away her age.

Matthew MacKay was not an active user of Facebook. He had very few posts and nothing recent. Katie was, however, able to find his wife's account. Her name was Laura Davis MacKay. She was also not an active user. She last posted a photo at Christmas time. It was a family photo of her, her husband, and two young men, each with a young woman standing next to them. One of the women was holding a baby. Judging by the positions in the photo, Katie guessed the young men were their sons, and the women were their sons' wives or girlfriends.

Katie checked her About page. "Look at this," she said. "She works as a firearms safety instructor at Shooters Plus Range and Supply Center. It also says she served in the U.S. Army."

Does it say what she did in the Army?

"No. Nothing about that."

"Whatever it was, we can assume she is good with a gun," Joe said. "It's very likely an Army-trained firearms instructor would be able to shoot two people in the heart with one bullet each."

"It looks like we found our killer," Katie said. "The question is, how do we prove it?"

"I don't know," Joe said. "All of our evidence is circumstantial. The video we have doesn't show the driver or the license plate number. It's too bad I didn't think to take pictures last night."

"Why don't you bring your camera tonight?"

"Tonight? You want to stake the place out tonight?"

"Sure. Why not? You didn't think we would stay here and have sex all day and all night, did you?" Katie asked.

"The thought did briefly cross my mind."

"Joe, if you help me crack this story, I promise I will wear you out when this is over. You will be begging me for a rest."

"You are quite the negotiator, Miss Katie. Who could refuse an offer like that?"

"Okay. So we're on the same page. I think we should call Garcia now."

Katie picked up her phone, dialed Lieutenant Garcia's number, and put it on speaker. "Hello, Katie," he said.

"Hello, Gabe. I'm here with Joe again. We have a question for you."

"I called you earlier, but there was no answer," Gabe said. "I learned that only one similar Corvette is registered in the area. That car is being restored and is not drivable."

"We're way ahead of you, Gabe," Joe said. "We followed the Corvette last night. MacKay's wife was driving it. She went inside the Williamses' apartment building for some unknown reason."

"I thought you were going to enjoy your day and let me take care of this," Gabe said.

"We did enjoy our day," Katie said, "but we saw the Corvette on the road after we picked up a pizza for dinner."

"How do you know it was MacKay's wife driving?" Gabe asked.

"We know because we followed her," Katie said. "She parked at the MacKays' apartment building and walked to the Williamses' building. We saw her walk by. The woman we saw looked exactly like MacKay's wife's Facebook profile photo. We also learned she is skilled with a gun."

"I've seen MacKay's wife a few times, but I don't personally know her. I did hear that she was in the first Gulf War."

"What was her job there?" Joe asked.

"I'm not exactly sure, but it had something to do with explosives. I was never in the Army, so I don't know what they call it, but from what I heard, it was like the bomb squad. Her team deactivated mines and IEDs and things like that."

"So she's an explosive expert. That's a scary thought," Joe said.

"What do we do now?" Katie asked. "Is there enough evidence to arrest her? Maybe you can scare her into talking."

"Are you asking me to arrest my Captain's wife? With the evidence we have? That might work for a common street thug, but I would surely lose my job if I dragged her into the police station."

"I see your point," Katie said. "I just hate the idea of waiting for her to kill someone else before we can do something about it."

"I hate it too, Katie, but my hands are tied here."

"What about Internal Affairs?" Joe asked. "If MacKay pulled you off the case to cover up his wife's crime, he is an accessory to murder. They could start their own investigation if you told them what you know."

"I'll think about it," Gabe said. "This feels like something that could blow up in my face."

"Okay, Gabe," Katie said. "We don't want to get you into hot water. We appreciate your help. Please let us know if you learn anything new."

"I will," he said. "You do the same."

After they said their goodbyes and hung up, Joe asked, "Do you think your station can run the story with the evidence we have?"

"Only if they want to get sued," Katie said.

"I'm not sure what else we can do right now."

Katie got up and sat on Joe's lap, facing him. She started unbuttoning Joe's shirt and said, "I think I can give you some of what I promised you now and the rest later."

"I think this is a good time to renegotiate," Joe said. "I want double."

***

A while later, as they lay in bed together, Katie said, "We have done so much together in such a short time. We now know who murdered the Williamses. We can't prove it yet, but I am confident we will be able to soon."

"Look at you being optimistic," Joe said.

"I think it's time we stop pretending everything will work out and discuss our future together," Katie said.

Joe felt backed into a corner and didn't know how to respond. He had hoped fate would intervene and solve the problem for him, but that hadn't happened yet. "Okay, Katie. Let's lay out the problem and see if we can find a solution. Essentially, we have three options."

"Three? I was thinking two, but okay. Let's start with the first one."

"Option one would be me staying here with you," Joe said. "In the plus column, I would be with you. That is a big plus. I might also be able to help you with future investigations. That is another plus. In the minus column is the fact that I am not a city boy. I'm happiest when I am near nature. I like getting away from people whenever I feel like it. When I say people, I don't mean you, but rather crowds of people. I also have the resort to think about."

"Okay," Katie said, "What about the second option?"

"Option two would be you coming to live with me in my cabin. I think you would like it there. You would be unable to work at the television station, which would be in the minus column, but there is so much to do there. We can ski in the winter and go on nature hikes in the summer."

"I would be bored without a career," Katie said.

"The resort needs a marketing manager. With your education and experience, I bet you could keep the place full all year."

"You are quite the salesman, Joe. What is this third option you have in mind?"

"We could just run away together. We can go to Europe or anywhere. Then, we can buy a condo in Florida, as we talked about. You are over thirty now, remember?"

Katie leaned over, kissed Joe, and said, "I love that you have a sense of humor, but right now, it's not making me feel better."

"What would make you feel better?" Joe asked.

"Let's get out of here. I know a nice little coffee shop that has great sandwiches."

"Sounds good. Let's go."

"I can't go like this. I have to get ready. Give me an hour," Katie said as she got out of bed.

"An hour? Really?"

"Okay, forty-five minutes. I need time to make myself look pretty."

"You're already beautiful. Just put some clothes on."

"You won't win this one, Joe."

Thirty-five minutes later, they were on the road. Katie drove into the city, and they parked in an area with several buildings that looked like apartments on top and retail stores on the bottom. The café was on the corner and had four tables on the sidewalk in front of the entrance. The weather was warm for January in Milwaukee, so all the tables were taken. Joe noticed three tables had dogs and figured the dogs, more than the weather, were the reason people chose those tables.

Inside, there were at least a dozen tables. Two tables were empty, but there were several people in line. Katie said, "I know you are not a coffee drinker, Joe, but they make a good iced coffee. They also have good Cuban sandwiches."

"I'll have what you're having, Katie."

Katie placed the order, and when the food was ready, they carried it to the only empty table they could find. Joe tasted the coffee and said, "This is surprisingly good for coffee."

"I had them make it with heavy cream for you. I'm trying to fatten you up."

"Keep trying," Joe said.

"Are you going to tell me you can't get fat either?"

"I don't know. I never tried."

"Nobody tries to get fat," Katie said, frustrated. "If I could just have a little of what you have, I would drop everything and come live with you."

"I will hold you to that," Joe said.

When they finished their lunch, Katie took Joe to the Public Market. He was impressed with how big the place was. Vendors were selling a wide variety of food. They passed a pastry shop and a candy store. There was a store with an array of honey flavors, along with real maple syrup. Joe spotted a deli and said, "Let's check this place out."

They stood in line behind several people. When they reached the counter, Joe ordered a small amount of several different types of lunchmeats and cheeses.

"What's that for?" Katie asked.

"If we are going to do a stakeout later, I thought it would be nice to bring along some sandwiches."

"You must have been a Boy Scout," Katie said.

"I was," Joe said. "It seems like a hundred years ago."

Katie rolled her eyes and said, "You are such an exaggerator. I doubt it was more than ninety-eight years ago."

Joe laughed and said, "It seems you have a sense of humor, too, Katie."

After the deli, they found a bakery where Joe bought a loaf of sourdough bread. There was also a produce stand where he picked up lettuce and tomatoes. "You are going all out on these sandwiches," Katie said.

"Only the best for my lady," Joe said.

They left the market and headed back to Katie's apartment. Once there, Joe spread everything out on the kitchen counter. He made four sandwiches and packed them in a cooler that Katie kept at the bottom of the pantry. He put water and ice packs in the cooler and closed it. Katie watched him and said, "It looks like we are going on a picnic."

"There's no rule that says a picnic has to be in the park. It can also be in a car while on a stakeout."

"I feel like I am working and going on a date at the same time."

"When work ceases to be fun, you should look for a new career," Joe said."

"It will be dark in an hour," Katie said. "Maybe we should get there early, just in case."

"I agree," Joe said. "Let's go."

Joe grabbed his camera bag, and they headed to the apartment. They parked across the street from the Williamses' apartment building when they arrived. It was still light, and they could see several people outside, including a couple of kids on a swing set at the house next to the apartment.

"We could be here all night," Joe said. "Are you prepared for that?"

"Well, I have to work tomorrow morning, so we should set a time limit. Let's call it a night if nothing happens by midnight."

"Okay, midnight it is," Joe said. "Are you hungry yet? Do you want a sandwich?"

"Of course, I want a sandwich. I wanted one while you were making them."

Joe got the cooler from the back seat and took out a sandwich and a bottle of water for Katie and for himself. Katie looked at the sandwich and said, "You didn't toast it."

"Really? That's what you have to say about it?"

Katie laughed, and Joe said, "Very funny. You better be careful. I know where your ticklish spots are."

Katie took a bite of her sandwich and said. "This is delicious. This is the best sandwich I've ever had."

"You're walking on dangerous ground, young lady."

"I'm not joking, Joe. This is very good. It was very thoughtful for you to put so much effort into it."

"I would do anything for you, Katie."

"You mean like sitting in a car all night waiting for something that may never happen."

"Okay, almost anything."

Katie slapped Joe on the arm and said, "Always with the jokes. I know you would do anything for me, and I love you for that."

Just then, a car drove down the street. Joe saw an old lady in the driver's seat. He said, "We should look at every driver that goes by. She may not drive the Corvette."

Katie leaned over and kissed Joe. She said, "If we watch every car, when will we have time to make out?"

Joe kissed her and said, "I think we can let a few get by."

Five hours later, Katie was sleeping with her head resting on Joe's shoulder. Joe saw a white sedan drive by. It was too dark to see the driver, but he remembered Gabe saying the captain drove a white sedan. He picked up his camera. He wanted to be prepared. When he did, Katie woke up and said, "What time is it?"

Joe looked at the clock on the dashboard and said, "A little after eleven."

"Did you see something?"

"I don't know. Maybe."

Joe set his camera to video mode and leaned his seat back a little. He set the camera lens on the edge of the door against the glass. He wanted to be ready.

"What did you see?" Katie asked.

"I saw a white sedan. I know millions of them are out there, but Gabe said that MacKay drives a car like that."

Katie and Joe both studied the sidewalk for any movement. Thirty seconds later, a figure appeared in the distance. Joe lined up his camera and started recording. Katie leaned her seat back, too, and they both tried to stay out of sight as best they could."

As the figure got closer, they could see it was Laura MacKay. She had something in each hand, but it was hard to tell what they were. She disappeared inside the apartment, and Joe and Katie looked at each other but said nothing. Joe kept the camera rolling. After five minutes, Laura MacKay exited the building. Joe recognized a wrench in her hand and noticed whatever was in her other hand was gone.

Joe removed the memory card from his camera, handed it to Katie, and said, "Here is your evidence. Keep it safe. I'm going inside. Stay here and call Garcia. Let him know what is going on. I'll see if I can figure out what she did."

Katie put the memory card in her coat pocket and zipped it closed while Joe got out of the car. "Be careful," she said.

"I'll be fine," he said and went inside the building. He stayed near the door and looked around, but saw nothing unusual. In front of him were stairs going up and down. He chose to go down. As he descended, he could smell something. When he reached the bottom, he knew what it was. It was the smell of gas.

He walked past an apartment on each side of the hallway. Beyond them were two more doors. The left door had an apartment number. The right door was open. He went to the open door. The light was off, but the hallway light illuminated it enough for him to see that it was a boiler room. There was a large boiler with pipes running seemingly everywhere. The smell of gas was almost overwhelming in the room. Joe had no plumbing experience, and there wasn't time to figure out what MacKay did.

"Joe?" came Katie's voice from outside the room. "Joe, where are you?"

Joe turned and saw Katie appear in the doorway. She reached her hand around to turn on the light, but Joe grabbed it and said, "It's gas. Any spark could set it off. What are you doing here? I told you to wait outside."

"I just came to see if you were okay. We need to warn these people."

"I'll do that. You go outside and call 911. Hurry."

Katie raced upstairs, and Joe started pounding on doors. "Gas leak! Get out now!" he yelled at each door. He made his way to the second and then the third floor. Once he was sure everyone was out or on the way out, he made his way downstairs.

When Katie got outside, she called 911. After a minute or so, she saw people exiting the building. She waited several minutes but didn't see Joe come out, so she went in to check on him just as the last resident left the building. Joe saw her come in as he reached the bottom of the stairs and yelled, "Katie! We gotta go!"

He grabbed her hand and pulled her out the door. They reached the top of the outside steps when the gas ignited and blew them clear of the building. They hit the ground hard on opposite sides of the sidewalk. Joe could feel dozens of pieces of debris embedded in his body. He was reminded of his war injuries. He looked up and saw Katie motionless, face down in the hard dirt.

"Katie!" he yelled. "Katie!"

The thought that she might be dead frightened him beyond measure. He tried to get up but couldn't. With much pain and great effort, he managed to crawl to Katie. When he reached her, he turned her head but saw no life in her. He put his hand on her cheek and closed his eyes. This time, he could feel her. He realized then that he had been thinking of her as a separate person. Now, he thought of her as part of himself. She was a part of him that he couldn't bear to lose. They were one person.

Katie came to suddenly. She could feel Joe like she did before, but this was even more intense. She thought maybe they had died and were in heaven. She could feel her injuries from the inside. She could also feel Joe's injuries. She knew he was in pain. She felt her body rejecting the debris embedded inside. She felt her body pushing out all the pieces. She then felt her blood clotting where it touched her skin. Suddenly, she no longer felt Joe. He was gone, and she was alone.

"Joe!" she yelled. She shook him, but he didn't respond. "Joe! God dammit! Don't you die on me!"

A paramedic knelt beside Joe. Another appeared next to Katie. He turned her head up and shone a light in her eyes. She turned back to Joe and cried, "Joe! Joe!"

# Chapter 18

The next thing Katie knew, she was in a hospital bed. Daylight shone through the window, so she knew it was the next day. A nurse monitoring her vitals noticed she was awake and immediately alerted a doctor, who entered the room. She looked to be around forty, with glasses and blond hair tied in a bun. "Good morning, Miss Kowalczyk," she said. "I'm Dr. Wilson. How are you feeling this morning?"

"I'm fine. Where's Joe?"

"Joe? Was that your companion?"

"Was? What do you mean by 'was?'"

"I'm sorry. That was a poor choice of words. I'm afraid your companion suffered more injuries than you did. He must have been behind you and protected you from the worst of the blast. He just came out of surgery. His injuries were substantial, and I'm afraid I don't know what his chances are. The surgeons did all they could; the rest is up to him."

Katie relaxed a little upon hearing that. "I want to see him," she said.

"I'm afraid he's in recovery right now."

"Please," Katie said.

The doctor thought for a moment and said, "Okay. I'll have someone bring you a chair. In the meantime, several people are here waiting to see you." She opened the door and motioned for them to come. Ashley, Bob Martin, Gabe Garcia, and Katie's parents entered the room as the doctor left.

Katie's mom hugged her and said, "We came as soon as we heard. We were so worried about you."

Her dad hugged her and said, "We are so happy you are okay."

Next, it was Ashley's turn, "Don't ever scare me like that again," she said.

Gabe spoke up, saying, "I hear you and Joe are heroes. You saved a lot of lives last night."

"At what cost?" Katie asked.

"You hit him with your car," Ashley said. "What's a little explosion? He's tough. He'll be fine."

Bob Martin looked surprised, "Is that how you two met? Is that why you were late on Monday?"

Katie sheepishly nodded.

"I guess he is tough," Bob said.

"Mr. Martin. Bob," Katie said. "Find out where they put my coat. Inside the pocket is evidence that will put Mrs. MacKay away. Please give a copy to Lieutenant Garcia. Also, I have enjoyed working with you and appreciate the opportunities you have given me, but please consider this my resignation."

"We will miss you at the station," Bob said, "but I understand."

"Gabe," she continued. "I don't know if your captain is a co-conspirator or an innocent dupe, but either way, I think they will be looking for a new captain, and I hope you get the job."

"If I do get the job," Gabe said, "I hope you and Joe would consider applying for the Police Academy. I could use good detectives like you."

"I appreciate the compliment, but I have something else in mind."

The door opened, and a nurse came in with a wheelchair. "Are you ready?" she asked.

Katie nodded, got out of bed, and sat in the chair. "Thank you all for coming," she said. "I have to go see Joe now."

The nurse pushed her into a room where Joe lay on a bed. Several wires were attached to his chest, a tube came out of his nose, and an IV hung nearby. The nurse wheeled Katie close to Joe and said, "I will give you a few minutes."

Katie held Joe's hand and said, "What the Hell is wrong with you, Joe? I should be there, and you should be here."

Joe opened his eyes and said, "I'm trying to rest. Rest is a time for healing."

Katie almost leaped out of her chair. She put her arms around Joe and said, "I was so scared. I thought you were dead."

"I remember a promise you made me."

"I remember, too," Katie said. "I quit my job today. My job is not important. It never was. I realized that when I thought I lost you. I also realized I was a hypocrite. I put my job first and you second. I won't do that again. My only request is that you get a bathroom put in that cabin of yours."

"I was thinking we need a bigger place. There is a house for sale down the road from the cabin. Perhaps we can look at it together in a couple of days when I'm better."

"I would love that, Joe, but you should slow things down. You don't want some hotshot reporter wondering how you got better so quickly."

The door opened, and Katie turned to see the nurse who had brought her there. She had an old woman with her. She was around eighty with a thin frame and short, curly white hair. "You must be Katie," she said. "I heard a lot about you. I'm Susan. How's my dad?"

"I'll be fine, Susan," Joe said.

Katie moved aside so they could see each other. "Oh, you're awake," Susan said. She moved in close and hugged him. "Michael and Eric are with me, but they had to wait outside."

She stood up, turned to Katie, and said, "Since Mom died, he's been a bit of a hermit. I'm glad he found someone who could get him out of his shell."

"I'm not a hermit, Susan."

\*\*\*

Two years later, Katie and Joe were at the reception desk of the Three Eagles Ski Resort when Michael came out of his office, followed by his accountant. He said, "We just finished our taxes, and profit is up over twenty percent from the year before."

"I think we can thank Katie for most of that," Joe said.

"I agree," Michael said. "I don't know what you are doing on the marketing end, Katie, but it's working.

The door opened, and Katie's parents walked in. Katie walked around to greet them. They hugged, and Katie said, "I'm so glad you could make it."

"Are you kidding?" her mom said. "We wouldn't miss our grandson's first birthday for the world."

She looked Katie up and down and added, "Married life must be good for you. You look younger every time I see you."

Katie glanced at Joe, who winked at her.

"Where is little Joey, anyway?"

"He is in the banquet room with my grandmother," Joe said.

They all went to the banquet room and found Susan sitting on a chair while little Joey admired the bow on one of his many gifts. Susan stood and said, "Hello again. I haven't seen you two since the wedding. Let me see if I can remember. Mary and Konrad, right?"

"My name is Karl, but that was close." Katie's father said.

They shook hands, and Mary said, "It is nice to see you again, Susan. You look wonderful." She then turned to look at Joey, "Oh, look at him. He is adorable."

Little Joey wore brown pants, tennis shoes, and a black shirt with "Daddy is older than Mommy" printed on it.

Joe asked, "Where did that shirt come from? He wasn't wearing that earlier."

"I might have bought it for him," Katie said.

"He fell and hurt his hand," Susan said. "I cleaned the wound and put a bandage on it, but he got blood on his shirt, so I changed it to one in his bag."

Katie knelt to look at Joey's hand. She pulled off the bandage and looked at the wound. "Look at this, Joe," she said.

Joe knelt next to her and looked at Joey's hand. The cut was barely visible, as if it had happened days ago. Joe looked at Katie and said quietly, "It appears I am no longer the last Healer."

I truly appreciate you taking the time to read The Last Healer. I hope you enjoyed following Katie and Joe on their first adventure.

I would be incredibly grateful if you left a review on Amazon, Goodreads, or wherever you purchased this book. Your thoughts help other readers discover the series and mean a lot to me as an author. Whether it's a few words or a detailed review, your feedback makes a difference.

Thank you again for your support. I couldn't do this without readers like you.

Charles Huss

# Books In This Series

## Last Healer Mysteries

Joe, a reclusive, ageless centenarian, meets Katie, an ambitious news personality with dreams of being an investigative reporter. Together, they solve crimes and explore the full potential of Joe's healing abilities while navigating the complexities of their intimate relationship.

## Book One - The Last Healer

On the eve of her thirtieth birthday, Katie, a television news reporter, unhappy with her career and her love life, decides to spend the weekend alone at a Wisconsin ski resort.

Joe is a man content to live a private life in his cabin in the woods. Since the death of his wife, he has avoided intimate relationships and prefers to keep a low profile to prevent people from learning of his unusual abilities.

On the way to the ski resort, Katie makes a wrong turn during a snowstorm and hits Joe with her car. Lost and with no cell signal, Katie tries to keep Joe alive until she can get help. During Joe's recovery, Katie learns his secret and soon helps to investigate his family's mysterious past while Joe helps Katie investigate a double murder. Love blossoms while they slowly unravel both mysteries, but danger lies ahead. Can Joe discover the full extent of his abilities before it is too late?

## Book Two - Last Rites

In this gripping sequel to "The Last Healer," Katie and Joe, fresh from their honeymoon, must race to Milwaukee to save the life of Katie's dear friend Ashley after she and her mother fall victim to a ruthless attack. With Ashley on the brink of death while a priest delivers Last Rites, her only chance for survival is Joe's remarkable healing powers.

What starts as a rescue mission turns into a murder investigation as they investigate the killing of Ashley's mother. While searching for the shooter, their investigation leads them to a chilling conspiracy centered on the city's homeless population. As they uncover more of the truth, they become targets as someone is determined to silence them. Will Katie and Joe find who is behind a series of murders, or will they become the next victims?

## Book 3 – Last Chance

In Book Three of the Last Healer Mysteries, Katie and Joe, after deciding to quit investigating murders, are thrust back into it when a man is murdered at Joe's resort. The victim is no ordinary man. He is a suspected jewel thief, believed to have hidden stolen jewels at the resort. While they struggle to handle all the treasure seekers, Katie and Joe debate how involved they should be in the murder investigation. They don't know the killer lurks in the background, taking orders from some of the most powerful people in Wisconsin while he waits for Katie and Joe to find what he is looking for.

## Book 4 - Last Flight

In book four of the Last Healer Mysteries series, Katie and Joe witness the deadly crash of a prototype aircraft and save the life of one of its occupants. After Joe discovers evidence of sabotage, Katie insists she is capable of investigating the crime despite being almost nine months pregnant.

Someone planted an explosive device in the aircraft, killing the company's founder and jeopardizing the struggling startup's future. Was the attack meant to destroy the company, or was it something more personal? As Katie and Joe hit one dead end after another, they learn the killer isn't finished.

With time running out, they race to save the next victim, but with people dying, a murderer on the loose, and Katie in labor, what's a Healer to do?

## Book 5 – Last Hope

In book five of the Last Healer Mysteries series, Katie and Joe are celebrating their son's first birthday when they learn the husband of Katie's childhood best friend has been arrested for murdering the small town's only police detective. They return to Katie's hometown, determined to find the real killer.

As they dig deeper, they uncover chilling ties between the detective's death and the recent killing of the mayor's daughter. It soon becomes clear someone will do anything to keep the truth buried.

# Other Books by Charles Huss

## Truth Be Told

Peter Beckett awoke 25 years ago with no memory of his past. Since then, he's been haunted by a gift he never asked for and doesn't want. People can't lie to him. To Peter, it feels like a curse that has left him isolated and feared by all who get to know him. Only his priest accepts him for who he is.

The FBI has been watching him, and they need his unique talent to track a deadly drug cartel that has infiltrated Milwaukee, fueling a dangerous spike of fentanyl overdoses. Rookie agent Hannah Meyers is assigned to recruit Peter, who is reluctant to help, but is intrigued by Hannah after she lies to him.

As the investigation deepens, details of Peter's former life emerge. With secrets unraveling and lives on the line, Peter must decide whether to return to the glorious life he once knew or give it all up for love.

## Saving Apollo

Apollo is no ordinary dog. Along with his sister, Athena, he was genetically modified to be smarter than a chimpanzee. When the lead geneticist quits over a dispute about the fate of the dogs, chaos erupts, and Apollo escapes, ending up on a small island off the Florida coast. There, he befriends twelve-year-old Ethan, who has just moved to the island with his dad, Ryan.

As they uncover Apollo's extraordinary ability to understand them, they also learn about the perilous fate that awaits him if he returns. With the help of their neighbor, Brooke, a local veterinarian, they devise a plan to save Apollo and Athena. Standing in their way is Jack Strauss, a former Marine and head of security at the lab that created Apollo and Athena.

"Saving Apollo" is a heartwarming, family-friendly story of friendship, love, and compassion.

## Falling Star

A meteorite crashes into the serene wilderness of a national park. In its aftermath, both people and animals succumb to aggressive behavior followed by death. Two rookies, FBI agent Beth Hartley and Park Ranger Mike Bauer, are put together to investigate the strange events.

Beth is tough as they come on the outside but vulnerable on the inside. After her last breakup, she has given up on men to focus on her career. Mike, a former military police officer, has developed trust issues and prefers his new career where he has no partner that he needs to rely on.

As their investigation brings them closer to the truth, they find themselves getting closer to each other. In a dangerous forest where every animal is a potential threat, and even the air could be toxic, their best chance for survival is a partner they can trust.

## Identity Crisis

After Alex Neumann agrees to participate in his father's groundbreaking memory recording experiment, he awakens years later to find he is not the man he used to be. He soon becomes a pawn in a deadly scheme involving a ruthless businessman, an Army general, and the President of The United States.

As Alex peels away layers of deception, his true identity slowly emerges, along with skills foreign to his old self. He will need all those skills and the help of friends he meets along the way to survive and turn the tables on his adversaries.

## Bad Cat Chris: The Baddest Cat You'll Ever Love

When Chuck volunteered to help a local cat shelter clean cages one morning, the last thing he expected was a kitten climbing up his back to perch on his shoulders, but that was the beginning of a relationship that would test the limits of human endurance and compassion. This is the story of Chris, a cat like no other who would turn the lives of Chuck and Rose upside-down while eventually showing them that bad can be good and love can come from the most unlikely places. This book is based on Chris's blog at BadCatChris.com and is a collection of sometimes serious but mostly humorous stories about the ups and downs of living with a bad cat.

# About The Author

Charles Huss was born and raised in the suburbs of Chicago but has lived most of his adult life in the Tampa Bay, Florida, area. He is a graduate of St. Petersburg College and is the writer of several books. He currently lives with his wife, Rose, and their three cats.

# Don't miss out!

Visit the website below and you can sign up to receive emails whenever Charles Huss publishes a new book. There's no charge and no obligation.

https://books2read.com/r/B-A-LHRY-NGOOC

BOOKS 2 READ

Connecting independent readers to independent writers.

Did you love *The Last Healer*? Then you should read *Last Rites*[1] by Charles Huss!

[2]

In this gripping sequel to "The Last Healer," Katie and Joe, fresh from their honeymoon, must race to Milwaukee to save the life of Katie's dear friend Ashley after she and her mother fall victim to a ruthless attack. With Ashley on the brink of death while a priest delivers Last Rites, her only chance for survival is Joe's remarkable healing powers.What starts as a rescue mission turns into a murder investigation as they investigate the killing of Ashley's mother. While searching for the shooter, their investigation leads them to a chilling conspiracy centered on the city's homeless population. As they uncover more of the truth, they become targets as someone is determined to silence them. Will Katie and Joe find who is behind a series of murders, or will they become the next victims?

Read more at charleshuss.com.

---

1. https://books2read.com/u/3RXNZn

2. https://books2read.com/u/3RXNZn

# Also by Charles Huss

**Last Healer Mysteries**
Last Chance
Last Flight
The Last Healer
Last Rites
Last Hope

**Standalone**
Identity Crisis
Falling Star
Saving Apollo
Truth Be Told

Watch for more at charleshuss.com.

# About the Author

Charles Huss was born and raised in the suburbs of Chicago but has lived most of his adult life in the Tampa Bay, Florida area. He is a graduate of St. Petersburg College and is the author of several books. He currently lives with his wife, Rose, and their two cats.

Read more at charleshuss.com.